"Nice Perfume.
It's Different From Your Usual."

Rina swallowed against the gasp of irritation that rose in her throat. She hadn't even thought about what perfume Sara had been wearing. It was yet another example of how careful she was going to have to be if she was to carry this off properly.

She turned and smiled at Rey, slipping on a pair of sunglasses as she did so, so he couldn't see the lie in her eyes. "It's something I picked up while I was away. Do you like it?"

From behind her, Rey leaned in and inhaled again, his lips mere centimeters from the curve of her neck.

"Mmm, yeah, I do."

A frisson of awareness shot down Rina's spine with the velocity of lightning, leaving a fierce sizzle throbbing in its wake.

What was it she had told herself only minutes ago? About handling things provided it didn't get too personal? Right now it looked as if that was to be her biggest obstacle, because despite everything, she was left fighting a desire to get very personal indeed.

Dear Reader,

One of the things I do before I start writing my books is spend time finding pictures of people who, to me, embody my characters. The picture I had in my mind of Reynard del Castillo was a good one, but the photo I found of the male model I ended up using as my inspiration for Reynard was beyond even my expectations. Choosing which photos *not* to use as visual prompts was a serious problem. I tell you, it's a tough job sometimes being a writer, but someone's got to do it.

In this story, Book #2 in WED AT ANY PRICE, set on my fictional Mediterranean island, Isla Sagrado, Reynard del Castillo gets more than he bargained for with his engagement to Sara Woodville. Especially when the fiancée in question turns out to be none other than her identical twin sister, Rina. This is the first time I've worked with a sister-swap story line and I loved working with both Rina's conscience and Reynard's determination to protect his family. I particularly loved the tug-of-war they each battled with as they found their path to love.

I hope you enjoy *Stand-In Bride's Seduction* and that you look forward to the next installment in the trilogy, where the youngest del Castillo brother, Benedict, finds that what he thought was lost forever was really just on the opposite side of the world. How he's going to keep it is quite another story.

Happy reading and very best wishes,

Yvonne Lindsay

YVONNE LINDSAY

STAND-IN BRIDE'S SEDUCTION

Published by Silhouette Books
America's Publisher of Contemporary Romance

SILHOUETTE BOOKS

ISBN-13: 978-0-373-73051-3

Recycling programs
for this product may
not exist in your area.

STAND-IN BRIDE'S SEDUCTION

Printed in U.S.A.

Books by Yvonne Lindsay

Silhouette Desire

*The Boss's Christmas Seduction #1758
*The CEO's Contract Bride #1776
*The Tycoon's Hidden Heir #1788
Rossellini's Revenge Affair #1811
Tycoon's Valentine Vendetta #1854
Jealousy & a Jewelled Proposition #1873
Claiming His Runaway Bride #1890
†Convenient Marriage, Inconvenient Husband #1923
†Secret Baby, Public Affair #1930
†Pretend Mistress, Bona Fide Boss #1937
Defiant Mistress, Ruthless Millionaire #1986
**Honor-Bound Groom #2029
**Stand-In Bride's Seduction #2038

*New Zealand Knights
†Rogue Diamonds
**Wed at Any Price

YVONNE LINDSAY

New Zealand–born to Dutch immigrant parents, Yvonne Lindsay became an avid romance reader at the age of thirteen. Now married to her "blind date" and with two surprisingly amenable teenagers, she remains a firm believer in the power of romance. Yvonne feels privileged to be able to bring to her readers the stories of her heart. In her spare time, when not writing, she can be found with her nose firmly in a book, reliving the power of love in all walks of life. She can be contacted via her Web site, www.yvonnelindsay.com.

This book is dedicated to the fabulous writers' organizations around the world, and the volunteers who run them, who provide support and encouragement and learning to wannabe writers everywhere.

One

"Rina! Over here!"

Sarina Woodville turned her head to the sound of her twin sister's voice. A huge smile spread across her tired features as she picked out the vibrant redhead in the crowd of faces in the airport's arrivals hall. Clearing customs and immigration had been smooth and efficient, a fact she was very grateful for at this stage of her journey. Tugging her suitcase along behind her, Rina crossed the short distance to her sister's waiting arms.

"It's so good to see you," Rina said.

"How was your trip? Absolute hell, I bet. It's so long, isn't it?" Sara bubbled along, not really listening for a response.

Despite how obviously happy her twin was to see her, Rina couldn't help but notice the strain on her face and the dark rings around her eyes.

"Sara, is everything okay? You're still all right with me staying with you, aren't you?"

She really hoped Sara hadn't changed her mind. When Rina's engagement had unexpectedly come to an ignominious end last week and Sara had suggested she come to Isla Sagrado for some much needed cosseting, she'd jumped at the chance to get away for a while. But now she was afraid she might be in the way. Sara had only recently become engaged herself, to some guy called Reynard del Castillo. Just privately, Rina thought the name a little on the pretentious side but then again, from what she'd heard from Sara, the family was virtually royalty here on this tiny Mediterranean island republic.

The del Castillos had sponsored the equestrian event trials Sara had participated in here after a successful tour in France. Her e-mails had been full of effusive praise for the beauty of the island—and the men on it. It hadn't taken a Mensa-rated IQ to see where her flighty sister was leading when her e-mails had mentioned Reynard del Castillo on several occasions. Their rapid engagement, though, had come as a huge surprise. This Reynard must be quite a man to have pinned Sara down.

Sara flashed her a weak smile. "Come to the cafe over here and we can talk."

"Can't we talk on the way to your place?" Rina asked, confused.

Right now she wanted nothing more than a shower, maybe a hot drink and then about ten or twelve uninterrupted hours of sleep. By tomorrow morning she was certain she'd be feeling human again. The journey between New Zealand and Isla Sagrado, with all its painfully necessary stopovers and airport transfers, was hitting around thirty-seven hours now, and counting. She was ready to drop on her feet.

"It's complicated and I don't have much time. I'm really sorry. I *will* explain later, I promise, but right now I have to get back to France."

"You what?" Rina's heart plummeted.

She knew Sara had recently been visiting some friends in the South of France, people she'd met on the event circuit, but had been due back today. Hence Rina's arrival here, timed to coincide with Sara's.

"Back to France? But didn't you fly in just now?"

Sara nodded, and wouldn't meet Rina's eyes. Instead she glanced at the departures board against the far wall.

"I did, but I'm just not ready to be back here yet. I thought I would be, but I need more time. Here." She reached into her handbag to grab an envelope and thrust it across the small, round table at Rina. "I wrote this for you just in case we missed one another this afternoon. Look, I'm really sorry. I wish I wasn't so strapped for time. I know you came here for support, but I really need *your* help. I've laid it all out in the letter and I promise to be back here for you as soon as I've sorted things out.

"Go to the cottage, I've given you the key in here." She tapped the envelope. "Settle yourself in, then when I get back we'll have a good old bitch-and-gossip session and get all our man-worries out of our systems, okay?"

The public address system suddenly crackled to life, announcing a final call for passengers to Perpignan.

"Oh, that's me. I'm so sorry, Reeny-bean," Sara said, using the pet name she'd always used when she needed to cajole or coerce her sister into a favor. "I know I said I'd be here for you but—"

Sara rose from her seat and reached forward to envelop Rina in her arms.

"I'll make it up to you soon, I promise. Love you!"

And then, she was gone. Stunned, Rina sat at the tiny

table and watched as her sister disappeared in the direction of her departure gate. When it finally penetrated her shell-shocked, jet-lagged, sleep-deprived mind that Sara had really gone and left her here, her fingers clenched reflexively around the envelope in her hand. The crinkle of paper reminded her that the only way she was going to get an answer from her sister right now was to open the envelope.

It was bulkier than she'd expected and she ripped away the seal to tip out the letter and a key—and something else that tumbled with a brilliant flash and landed on the coffee-cup-rim-stained table in front of her. Rina reached quickly to pick it up, barely stifling a gasp of shock as she did so. A massive princess-cut diamond solitaire set on an ornately chaste platinum band winked back at her.

It was typical Sara to put something so valuable in something as innocuous and insecure as an envelope. Rina stifled the sudden surge of irritation that flooded through her at Sara's careless actions, and unfolded the single sheet of paper. As she read her sister's looped handwriting, her fingers fisted tight around the ring in her hand.

Rina groaned out loud. Sara hadn't. She couldn't have. It was beyond belief and way beyond anything her sister had ever done before. No wonder she hadn't wanted to admit any of this face-to-face and had run the instant she'd had the opportunity. Rina scoured the words again, hoping against hope that she'd misread something, but no.

Darling Rina, I'm so sorry I can't be there with you. I know it's a tough time for you but at least you're away from him—and can take some time to heal. Thing is, I think I've made a big mistake and I really need some space to think long and hard about whether I'm doing the right thing. Please, can you be me for a few days while I sort things out? Reynard will never need to know. Just put on my engagement ring and wear some of my stuff—you know, like we used to before we grew up. Well, before you grew up anyway. My maturity is probably still under question.

Sara went on to list a few hints and tips about Reynard, things like how they'd met, what his favorite beverage was, where they'd been together.

Beneath her exhaustion and the shock of her sister's outrageous request, Rina felt anger begin to swell from deep inside.

How dare Sara ask her to do this? Had she no compassion for anyone but herself? How could she expect her twin, fresh from a painful broken engagement, to slide straight into another and pretend to be someone she wasn't? It was totally and completely wrong. Let alone what it was expecting of Rina, it certainly wasn't fair to Reynard del Castillo, either.

Rina crushed the letter in her hand as her anger inflamed and grew. The words Sara had used imprinted on her mind.

I think I've made a big mistake.

She heard almost exactly the same words play in her head from when she'd last heard them. Not from Sara, but from her ex-fiancé, Jacob.

Despite the warmth in the airport terminal, Rina felt suddenly and unutterably cold. She was back there in that restaurant. Their favorite. Sitting across from the man she'd planned to spend the rest of her life with and hearing him tell her that he had fallen in love with someone else. How he'd been putting off telling her for months but with their wedding only a week away, he could put it off no longer.

Rina shook her head to rid it of the images lodged there. After the deception Jacob had practiced all those months, the thought of deceiving someone else made her feel physically ill. There was no way she was doing this. Not even for her twin. No way.

She shoved the letter, key and ring into the envelope and pushed them deep inside her handbag before hoisting the bag back onto her weary shoulder and getting up from the table. She reached for the handle on her suitcase and pulled it along behind her. She was going to find a taxi, go to the cottage where Sara had been staying, get showered, get dressed and, somehow, find this Reynard del Castillo and tell him what her sister was obviously too afraid to. No one deserved to be lied to as Sara had suggested. No one.

Reynard del Castillo studied the court report that had sat on his office desk now for six months. He'd kept it there as a reminder to be ever-vigilant of the opportunists who frequently targeted his family as a fast ticket to easy street.

He opened the report and stared at the name marked in bold ink. Estella Martinez. The woman had worked for him here in his office. Vivacious, beautiful and intelligent, he'd almost been tempted into indulging in an affair with her. Almost, but not quite, because instinct warned him she was not what she painted herself to be. When Estella had attempted to stage a scene between them, one where he would be seen to be breaching employer-employee protocols, he'd spun into action to ensure that her claims of sexual harassment and her offers to keep things quiet—both from his family and the tabloids, for several hundred thousand Euros—fell flat in the dust.

Estella Martinez's pitiful grasping attempt at her

moment of fame, her attempts at extortion—all of it had been exposed in the closed court trial. He'd used every one of his contacts and the weight of his family name and position to see that her charges were brought before the Court within the minimum amount of time and that there was no public access to either the proceedings or the results of those proceedings.

To avoid a prison sentence for the extortion attempt, she had agreed to the gag clause his attorneys had so cleverly worded as well as the restraining order to remain well away from Isla Sagrado and any member of the del Castillo family, wherever they might be traveling.

He slid the concisely written papers back into the envelope in which they'd been delivered and sent the entire package through his shredder. There, gone as effectively as she had been escorted to the airport and off the island. He needed no such reminders now.

While the experience had left a bad taste in his mouth, his recent engagement to Sara Woodville was all the more sweet. She made few demands upon their relationship, which was exactly the way he wanted it to be, and helped to serve the purpose for which the engagement was intended: to keep his grandfather off his back about the curse of the governess. The old story of the curse dated back hundreds of years to a time of myths and superstitions which was where, in Reynard's opinion, nonsense like that belonged. But his grandfather, *Abuelo,* had recently fixated on it, and to ensure the old man stopped worrying about Rey and his brothers being the last of the family line, as the curse predicted, Reynard and his brothers had taken steps to ease his fears.

It had been bad enough when *Abuelo*'s unnecessary tension and worry had led to a stroke last month. His manservant had acted swiftly and *Abuelo* had received the vital medical care he needed to begin a strong recovery. Neither Rey nor his brothers, Alexander and Benedict, wanted to go through that again. They'd already resolved to do whatever it took to put the family patriarch's mind at rest, to ensure his final years were as comfortable as they could be.

Alex had gone so far as to revisit a twenty-five-year-old engagement promise made when he was only a boy and the woman involved was but three months old. Rey smiled as he thought of his new sister-in-law, Loren. She'd looked so frail and feminine—so young when she'd returned to Isla Sagrado to be Alex's bride. Who could have known a backbone of pure steel ran through her tiny frame?

She'd fought hard for her marriage. Fought and won. And strangely enough, she and Alex no longer scorned the idea of the curse. If anything, in their happiness, they were all the more determined for him and Benedict to settle down.

Settling down wasn't really something Reynard was ready for, but in the meantime, being engaged to Sara was working out quite nicely when it came to soothing *Abuelo*'s mind. And that, ultimately, was all Reynard was concerned with. Reynard would do whatever it took to protect his family—to ease every fear and to eliminate, utterly and completely, any threat. And women like Estella Martinez—well, they would get their just deserts every time.

Sarina lifted her face to the warm Mediterranean sun as she stepped outside Isla Sagrado's airport terminal. The contrast between the golden kiss of heat on her cheeks and the icy chill of rain, sleet and snow back home in the South Island of New Zealand was unbelievable. No wonder

Sara had chosen to stay here rather than come home to a southern hemisphere winter.

And if all had gone as it was supposed to, Rina would have been not far from here on a Greek island for her honeymoon. She remembered going to the travel agency with Jacob and poring over the brochures, weighing and balancing the charms of each destination to find the perfect place to celebrate the start of their new life together.

Rina absently rubbed the ring finger of her left hand with her thumb. An old habit, and one she would train herself to stop as she became all too aware of the deficit there and the faint indentation in her skin.

She tilted her head back a little, and closed her eyes against the brightness of the sun. Funny how her eyes watered even behind her sunglasses.

So what if Jacob had wanted someone more spontaneous, someone who wasn't afraid to spice things up? Rina bit back tears at the memory of the emotional hurt he'd inflicted. And here she'd thought she'd chosen a life partner who was stable and secure—someone the complete antithesis of her parents and their fiercely intense, competitive and oftentimes combative relationship. Just went to prove how wrong a girl could be. She'd have felt better if she and Jacob *had* fought—if he'd simply told her that she wasn't what he wanted, rather than stringing her along for all that time, long after he'd stopped loving her.

Rina forced from her mind the memory of Jacob's unrepentant and abrupt withdrawal from the relationship they'd developed over the past five years. She'd promised herself she wouldn't shed another tear over him. And she wouldn't. Not a single one.

She swallowed hard against the lump in her throat. Why were promises so darn hard to keep?

The crowd of travelers she'd arrived with had long since

dispersed, and the sidewalks outside the terminal building were nearly empty. Worse, so were the taxi stands. Half an hour later Rina was beginning to wilt as the concentrated afternoon heat continued to build around her. Mindful of her fair skin—the curse of a natural redhead—she'd sought some shade near the side of the building.

A trickle of perspiration ran down Rina's back, as she flicked another glance at her watch—a gift from Sara and her only really frivolous piece of jewelry with its crystal embedded bezel and bracelet-style strap. Finally, thankfully, a green-and-white taxi pulled up. Tucking her shoulder bag securely against her side, Rina tightened her grip on the extended handle of her practical black suitcase and rolled it to the curbside.

"The Governess's Cottage, please," Rina said through the open passenger window.

Was it her imagination or did the driver surreptitiously cross himself as he got out of the taxi and walked around to lift her suitcase into the trunk of his car? Either way, she was too tired to care right now. She could only focus on one thing. Sorting out this wretched mess her sister had left her in.

Rina watched the departing taxi speed down the road for a few minutes, more than a little startled by the haste with which the driver had taken off. Goodness only knew why he was in such a hurry.

She grabbed her suitcase handle for what she hoped would be the last time in the next four weeks and trudged wearily through the pretty iron gate set within a stone wall that surrounded the cottage. "Quaint" really was the only word to describe the ancient structure, Rina decided as she followed the path to the tiny front porch with its stone steps worn by the passage of years of foot traffic.

Pale ocher-plastered brick here and there, the plaster crumbling away, revealing the ancient brick beneath—and with a darker orange tiled roof, it looked like an old-fashioned watercolor. Deep-set mullioned windows, sashed with faded blue wooden trim, gave an insight into sparse, but adequate, furnishings inside. Not entirely Spanish in style, yet not entirely French either, the cottage was a delightfully eclectic mixture of both.

Inside, she thought she could hear a phone ring before the strident chime shut off abruptly for a few moments then started all over again.

Rina dug in her handbag for the envelope Sara had left her. The heavy old key fit neatly into the ancient black lock, and the door swung smoothly open. The telephone, coincidentally, fell silent once more as she stepped inside.

She didn't take so much as a second to admire the exposed beam ceiling of the main rooms of the cottage, nor the pristine perfection of the charming blue and white tiled bathroom. And she didn't allow herself more than a single longing glance at the all-too-tempting bed in the room where she'd stowed her suitcase. She was a woman on a single-minded mission. To tell Sara's fiancé exactly what she'd done. Surely he'd be reasonable. After all, they'd met and become engaged in such a short space of time. They barely knew one another. A certain amount of second thought was bound to occur.

After her shower, Rina grabbed the first thing off the top of her open suitcase and dragged it over her barely dry body, and headed into the open-plan sitting room where she searched for a phone.

Ten minutes later she had exactly what she needed. Thanking Isla Sagrado's multilingual culture, and the high profile of the del Castillo family, not to mention the helpfulness of the information operator, for making the process so straightforward, she made another quick call and ordered a taxi to collect her and take her into the city, Puerto Seguro, and Reynard's offices.

By the time Rina arrived at the tasteful high-rise in the downtown section of the port city, she was running on pure nerves. Having been the recent recipient of such a break in relations, she was wary of how to approach this. What did you say to someone you'd never met before when you wanted to tell him that his engagement was very likely on shaky ground?

She smoothed trembling hands over the sleeveless beige silk dress she'd pulled on in such a hurry and hoped her hair wasn't already escaping the casual twist. She'd secured it with a couple of topaz-colored jeweled clips she'd found scattered, in typical Sara-like fashion, on the bathroom vanity.

A quick scan of the floor directory next to the bank of elevators gave her the last bit of information she needed. Rina stepped into one of the elevator cars and pressed the button for the twenty-first floor. Her stomach lurched as the car started its upward journey, and all the while she ran through her head what she needed to say.

The corridor that faced her as she stepped out was vast and empty. The muted tones of elegant piped music filtered through discreetly placed ceiling speakers. Directly ahead of her was a matched pair of large wooden doors, each one displaying an ornate carving that was, no doubt, the del Castillo family crest. Rina stepped forward and ran her fingertips over the raised edges of the stylized shield divided into three sections. In one was an intricately carved sword, in another a scroll or parchment of some description and the bottom section held an ornate heart. Her patchy Spanish translated the words.

Honor. Truth. Love.

She swallowed. If the man she was coming to see lived by the ancient code of his family, then she was definitely doing the right thing by coming here and telling him the truth. It was the only thing she could do.

Rina pushed against the brass doorplate at the very same moment the door in question swung abruptly away from her. With all her energy moving forward, she stumbled and suddenly fell against an immovable rock of a hard male body clad in a perfectly tailored charcoal gray suit.

Large, warm hands swiftly cupped her elbows and steadied her. Balanced on her feet now, Rina summoned a smile and looked up. Instantly, her heart skittered in her chest as she took in the perfection of male beauty in the face above hers.

A broad, tanned forehead, strong dark brows over clear hazel eyes edged with short, dark lashes. A perfectly balanced face bisected by a straight nose that had obviously never been on the wrong end of a tackle in a rugby game, and finely chiseled lips that were even now curving in a smile that held a strange combination of recognition and relief.

"Thank God you're here," he murmured, his voice a deep caress that she felt as though it was a stroke of velvet across her skin.

"Mr. del Castillo. Your brother says he'll meet you at the hospital," the receptionist at the vast modern desk behind him said.

The young woman's words sank slowly into Rina's mind. Mr. del Castillo? This man, who looked like he'd be better suited to the cover of *GQ* magazine than a conference room, was her sister's fiancé, Reynard del Castillo?

Two

Before she realized what was happening, Rina found herself spun around and, her hand firmly locked in his, was marched swiftly toward the elevators.

"Sara! I've been trying to reach you for the past hour! I tried both your cell and your home phone because I wasn't sure you were back on the island. I don't know why you refused to tell me the details on your flight information. I could have picked you up from the airport. Why didn't you call me?"

"I—" she began. Her mind raced to catch up with him. Cell phone. Of course, Sara must be ignoring his calls. With her own number being New Zealand based, on global roaming, she knew she couldn't just say she'd changed numbers. *Think,* she told herself, *what would Sara do or say?* Rina latched onto the easiest response. "I'm sorry—I lost my phone while I was away. You know what I'm like."

"It doesn't matter now. I'm just glad you're here."

"But I—"

The look on his face sent a chill down through her. His eyes, which only a moment ago had been warm and welcoming, were suddenly bleak—a small frown creasing the smooth skin between his brows.

"I've got bad news. Benedict's been involved in an accident. Alex just called me. We're meeting him and *Abuelo* at the hospital. Thank goodness you came here, saves time for us both."

"Benedict?"

"The idiot." Reynard shook his head slowly. "You know how he drives. Seems the coast road out to the vineyard got the better of him, and that high performance pile of metal he calls a car."

"Is he okay?"

"No, he's not. We're not sure how long he was trapped in the car but it took emergency services nearly an hour to free him from the wreck. He's in surgery now."

Reynard's voice broke on the words and Rina instinctively curled her fingers tighter around his.

"I'm sure he'll be okay," she said with as much calm encouragement as she could muster.

Inside, though, her stomach knotted on the news. How on earth could she tell Reynard that she wasn't who he thought she was now? Benedict was the younger of the del Castillo brothers; she remembered that much from one of Sara's e-mails. She also remembered Sara mentioning that Benedict ran the winery division of the family business.

"I'm glad you're here," Reynard said, his hand all but squeezing hers now.

"I'm glad I'm here, too," she whispered in response, and in a strange way she really was.

The last thing he needed right now was an absentee

fiancée. Tomorrow would be soon enough to tell him the truth, once they knew that Benedict would be all right.

Reynard fell silent for the balance of the journey in the elevator. Rina could feel the tension and worry radiating off him in tangible waves and her heart twisted. She knew how she'd be feeling right now if it was Sara in the same position as Benedict. She'd barely be able to function.

Finally, the elevator doors sprang open to reveal a basement parking garage. Reynard reached into a trouser pocket and she saw the lights flash on a vehicle across the way. Even in the basement lighting, the low sleek car shone as if its surface was mirror finished. The rearing horse symbol on the front grill spoke to its expensive origins.

Confusion swirled around her. So far Reynard del Castillo hit every one of her sister's hot buttons. He was deliciously tall, exquisitely handsome and clearly money was no object. Rina had been unable to detect a single thing about him that wouldn't appeal to her sister on any level. So why was Sara wondering if she'd made a mistake? And why did she feel she had to leave to figure things out? It wasn't like Sara to run away from anything, either. She was usually more up-front about things than this. So why had she done so?

Despite his obvious anxiety about his brother, and his eagerness to get to the hospital, Reynard took the time to open the passenger door for her and waited until she was settled before closing her door and coming around to the driver's side. It took her by surprise. She was staunchly independent, and more than used to taking care of herself. She expected and administered equality in all the spheres of her life. However, the old-fashioned courtesy was strangely appealing.

And that wasn't all that was appealing about the man. In the close confines of the car, her senses became finely tuned to everything about him. The warmth that emanated from his body despite the car's air-conditioning, the capable movement of his hands on the steering wheel and the gear stick as he maneuvered out of the car park and into the blinding sunlight outdoors—not to mention the subtle blend of his fragrance.

She closed her eyes and slowly inhaled, mentally picking apart the different layers of the scent. It reminded her of the decadence of consuming a succulent mango, slice by luscious slice, and underlying that sensual fruitiness was another scent. Something spicy. Patchouli, maybe? Whatever it was, it was doing crazy things to her insides. Things that her insides shouldn't be doing given that she'd just been cast off by her own fiancé and was thinking these thoughts about her sister's!

Rina forced her eyes open. This was ridiculous. She'd never been the type to be so easily swayed by a man's appearance and presence. Passionate attraction went against every reasonable, logical instinct she had—and it scared her a little. Even at the height of her relationship with Jacob, when she'd agreed to spend the rest of her life with him, she'd never felt as drawn to him as she now did to the stranger sitting beside her.

She tried to shake it off. She was just overtired…and maybe a little emotionally vulnerable, after everything that had happened. Yes, that was definitely what was wrong with her. She'd get some sleep tonight and tell Reynard the truth tomorrow, and everything would go back to normal. She allowed her lips to part and forced herself to breathe lightly through her mouth in a vain attempt to rid herself of the disquieting sensation burgeoning to life deep inside her. Suddenly, telling him the truth tomorrow seemed a long, long time away.

When they pulled up outside the hospital, Rina alighted

from the car before Reynard could come around to her side
and open the door for her. He did, however, ensure her hand
was tucked in the corner of his arm as they walked toward
the hospital doors.

It was all too easy to see why her sister had fallen so
quickly for this man. He was what they'd always referred
to between them as the whole package. She was no shortie,
standing at five feet ten inches in bare feet, but he topped
that by almost half a foot and had an air of command
intriguingly entwined with an aura of sophisticated
sexuality. It was enough to make a grown woman's mouth
water.

Focus, Rina growled to herself, as they entered the
pristine hospital reception area and Reynard made
straight for the elevators. All the signs here were in three
languages—Spanish, French and English—so she knew
they were headed for the surgical floor.

Sudden nerves assailed her. What if another member
of the family recognized her for a fraud? What would she
do then? She forced herself to breathe calmly. Why should
anyone suspect anything? she rationalized. If Reynard
himself, supposedly Sara's fiancé, didn't immediately see
the difference, then it made sense that no one else would,
either.

On the surgical floor they were shown to a private waiting
room. Immediately Rina spotted another handsome man
who she assumed was Reynard's elder brother, Alexander.
He stood near a window, his arm around a slender woman
of average height, offering her comfort even as his own
face bore the ravages of the worry they were all going
through. Although his hair was darker than Reynard's, the
family resemblance was still incredibly strong. On closer
inspection, Rina realized that, converse to her original

impression, the woman at his side was supporting him, rather than the other way around.

As soon as Alex saw his younger brother, he pulled away from his wife and came across the room. The affection the del Castillo brothers bore for each other was evident in the way they clasped in a long and silent embrace.

"Any news?" Reynard said as they pulled apart.

"Nothing," Alex said, his voice hoarse.

"The doctor said it could be a few hours," the other woman volunteered gently. Suddenly, she seemed to notice Rina standing near the door and crossed the room toward her. "You must be Sara. I'm so sorry our first meeting should be under these circumstances."

First meeting? Had Sara never met Reynard's family?

"She's only just returned from visiting friends in France. I haven't even given her time to take a breath yet." Reynard turned to Rina and pulled her to his side. "Alex, Loren, this is Sara Woodville, my fiancée."

"Welcome to the family," Alex said, taking her hand and leaning in to kiss her on the cheeks in European fashion. "As Loren said, I'm sorry we had to meet you like this, but I am glad you are here for Reynard."

"Thank you," she answered, but before she could say any more a commotion outside the waiting room distracted them.

A volley of voluble Spanish rent the air as the door opened. The del Castillo imprint was obvious on the face of the elderly gentleman who pushed into the room, leaning heavily on a highly polished wooden cane, soon followed by a middle-aged man who looked both worried and apologetic at the same time.

"I went to visit him at the nursing home to tell him the news in person, and he took my car keys and tried to hijack my car. I tried to stop him, *señors,* but he would not listen," the younger man said. "He said he would drive himself here if I did not bring him."

"Listen? Pah!" the white haired gentleman spat. "You think I am too old to give support to my grandchildren when they need me?"

"Don't worry, Javier, *Abuelo* will be fine with us. Why don't you see if you can find us all some decent coffee to drink, hmm?" Reynard suggested while smoothly stepping forward and taking his grandfather's arm.

"I know everyone else's preferences but, *señorita,* how do you take your coffee?" Javier asked.

"Strong and milky, thank you," Rina replied with a smile.

"You are forgetting your manners," the old man chastised his grandson. "Who is this young lady?"

His slightly quavering voice in heavily accented English belied the sharply inquisitive gleam in his eyes as he assessed Rina. For a moment she wondered if he could see right through her, see the falsehood she was perpetrating by masquerading as her twin.

"This is Sara Woodville, my fiancée," Reynard responded smoothly.

"It's about time she came back. I was beginning to think she was a figment of your imagination. The governess, she won't wait, you know. You mark my words. This accident of Benedict's," he stated as he waved a mottled hand through the air, "it is no accident, I tell you."

"*Abuelo,* enough!" Alex's voice was sharp. "Benedict endangered his own life every time he got behind the wheel of a car. It was bound to catch up with him sooner or later. It had nothing to do with—"

"You can deny it all you wish, my boy, but the facts remain in front of your face as clear as your nose. Now, where is my grandson? I wish to see him."

He imperiously stamped the cane he clutched in one gnarled hand on the vinyl floor, and Rina suddenly realized why the brothers had not wanted him at the hospital. He had no idea just how seriously hurt Benedict was.

She looked from the elderly man to his two grandsons, especially Reynard. His face was a mask of concern, his hazel eyes clouded. Clearly Benedict's injuries were life threatening. Why else would he and Alex be so determined to keep the information from their grandfather? And now, with him demanding to see his youngest grandson, and with the obvious respect they had for him so apparent in their demeanor, how could they tell him the truth?

Without a second thought, Rina stepped forward and tucked her hand in the crook of the older man's arm.

"Mr. del Castillo, I've been traveling all day and I'm exhausted. I need to sit down. Why don't you come and sit with me over here on one of these chairs and we'll get to know one another a little better?"

It wasn't an exaggeration. She *was* exhausted, and she'd been traveling, or on her feet now, for the better part of two days.

"What is this?" he bristled.

Rina immediately threw a worried glance toward Reynard who merely lifted his eyebrows a fraction.

"I'm sorry. Did I say something wrong?" she apologized.

"Rey, explain the meaning of this. Why does your fiancée call me *Meester* del Castillo?"

A small smile pulled at the sensual curve of Reynard's lips, giving Rina little insight into what had upset his grandfather.

"Should I have said *señor?* I'm sorry, my Spanish is—" she broke off. What if Sara's Spanish had improved past the basic minimum they'd both learned in their late teens on their big overseas experience?

"It is my mistake—I should have introduced the two of you properly instead of only doing half a job. Sara, this is my grandfather, Aston del Castillo," Reynard interjected.

"You must call me *Abuelo*," the old man replied, with a sudden twinkle in his eye. "If you're serious about marrying my grandson, that is."

Across the room Rey watched Sara blanch at his grandfather's words, and felt a brief surge of panic. Surely she wouldn't expose the capricious nature of their engagement now. He knew they'd entered into the thing as a bit of a lark, neither of them serious about it for now. Even Sara had said they should see where the wind blew them.

Her attitude had been what had made her perfect for the role as his fiancée. He'd needed an engagement that would require little true commitment from him while still keeping his grandfather off his back about getting married. He doubted that Sara had any more intention of them actually getting married right now than he did, himself. If *Abuelo* would just stop harping on about that wretched curse, they could all get back to normal again. And then, in a few months, he and Sara could part ways gracefully and without any hard feelings.

Of course, *Abuelo* was arguing even harder in favor of the curse now in light of the success of Alex and Loren's marriage. There was no denying that things had improved financially for the family business and economically on Isla Sagrado as a whole, even in the short time since the two had married, supporting *Abuelo*'s claims that marriage for all three of the brothers would break the curse, and bring prosperity back to the family.

Reynard still had his doubts though, about the curse of the governess. *Abuelo* had become unhealthily obsessed with the subject in recent months, even claiming to see her ghost. If the old man were to be believed, the scorned woman's final words to her del Castillo lover were solely responsible for every sudden death in the family, not to mention the downturn in the economy of Isla Sagrado. In itself, the thought was ridiculous, but Reynard and his brothers loved their grandfather deeply and had been prepared to do whatever it took to ensure his final years remained happy. Even if, on Reynard's part, it meant faking an engagement.

Suddenly Rey became aware of the extended silence in the room. He stepped forward to Sara's other side and kissed the tip of her lightly freckled nose, and was amused to see a faint flush of color flood her cheeks.

"Of course she's serious about marrying me, *Abuelo*. Who wouldn't want to be a del Castillo bride?"

"Bueno," the old man said then nodded and allowed himself to be drawn over to a bank of chairs in the room where he pulled Sara down alongside him.

Before long, their heads were together and Rey felt a sense of reprieve that his grandfather was distracted, at least for now. He moved over to Alex and Loren.

"She did that well," Alex commented, nodding to where Sara and their grandfather were conversing in a combination of Spanish and English.

Rey nodded, "Thank goodness. What were you going to tell him?"

Alex's face grew bleak. "The truth?"

"No," Loren murmured. "You can't. Not while he's still recovering from his stroke. He's not even well enough to be back home at the castillo yet. I'd be terrified he'd suffer a setback and never be allowed home—and you know what that would do to him."

"You're right," Rey agreed. "We don't want a repeat of that night."

"So what then? Keep him waiting with us until the surgeons are finished?"

"Surgeons?"

Rey felt ill. So there was more than one surgeon working on his brother. Working to save his life. The deep hollow ache that had manifested in his chest during Alex's first call sharpened and ached that little bit harder. He sent a silent prayer that his brother's strength and health would be enough to see him through this and that the skill of Isla Sagrado's best doctors would ensure his return to his family fold, where he belonged.

He gathered his fears in a tight knot and thrust them to the back of his mind.

"Did they say how long?"

Alex shook his head. "Could be hours yet."

Rey looked back toward Sara. "*Maybe* if Sara takes him, *Abuelo* will agree to go back to the home. Javier can drive them both and then take her back to the cottage."

"It's a good idea, but," Alex suggested as he curled his arm just that little bit tighter around his wife's slender waist, "are you sure you don't need her here?"

Need her here? Rey's mind was fogged for a moment but then he realized what his brother was getting at. Of course, under normal circumstances, if his had been a normal engagement, he'd want his fiancée here with him. But would Sara agree to play along? The one time she'd needed medical attention during the event trials where he'd met her, she'd all but run screaming from the first aid tent. All because they'd wanted to examine her when she'd bumped her head after fainting in the heat. He'd have guessed that, under any circumstances, a hospital was the last place on earth she'd choose to be. Besides, their relationship was hardly one where he would expect her emotional support at a time like this.

He quickly recovered his scattered thoughts. "Perhaps later. She's tired, just returned from Perpignan." *And God only knows where else judging by the exhaustion dragging at her lithe body.* "I didn't even give her time to say hello before we were on our way here. I'll suggest it to them after Javier has brought coffee."

It must have taken a minor miracle but Javier eventually returned with a series of steaming hot paper cups in varying sizes and handed each to its recipient, the shortest and darkest brew going to *Abuelo*.

"Ah, thank goodness. Finally, a decent cup of coffee." The old man sighed his pleasure as he savored the aromatic beverage.

"I thought it would be okay, just this once," Javier said by way of explanation to the brothers. "What they serve him in the convalescent home is…" Javier's expression left nothing to the imagination.

"That's fine," Rey replied and watched as Sara lifted the top off her cup and blew on the milky contents before taking a sip. *Abuelo* had distracted him when she'd given Javier her coffee order earlier, but now Rey looked at her in surprise. He knew for a fact that she took her coffee black, when she drank it. In the past couple of weeks, though, she hadn't touched any, saying she was on a health kick or something like that. Looked like the health kick was over, if the way she obviously enjoyed the coffee now was any indicator.

Rey watched as her throat slowly swallowed, the muscles moving sinuously beneath her pale skin, and suddenly he was jolted with a burst of sexual awareness that completely blindsided him.

Their relationship to date had been more platonic than passionate. Sure, they'd exchanged a few kisses in the moonlight, but overall he hadn't been fixated on getting her into his bed. They had fun together—kept things light and carefree—and that was the way he'd planned on keeping it before eventually carefully deconstructing the engagement and withdrawing with no hurt feelings. Right now, though, he wanted nothing more than to lose himself, and what was happening to his family, in the soft scents of her skin and the sensations of being entwined with her body.

She looked up at him over the rim of her cup, her gray eyes widening at what he could only assume was the burning hunger reflected in his own. Her hand shook slightly as she tipped her cup straight again and lowered it onto the table next to her. Her pink tongue swept away the trace of moisture left behind by the coffee on her lips.

Inside, whatever had taken hold of him tightened and sharpened into something totally inappropriate for a hospital waiting room. Remembering that somewhere on this floor his younger brother fought for his life beneath a surgeon's blade brought Rey painfully back into the here and now.

"*Querida,* you look weary. Perhaps you should go back to the cottage. I can call you there—let you know when we hear any news." Before she could answer he turned to his grandfather. "Would you escort her back for me, *Abuelo*? I promise, we will let you know every ten minutes, if necessary, if there are any updates, but for now, I would prefer it if Sara was taken home. Clearly she's worn out and needs rest."

He looked at Sara, his eyes locking with hers and willing her to agree, as he waited for his grandfather's blustering refusal. He saw the instant she understood his intention and watched as she turned to the old man.

"Would you? I always feel better if someone sees me to the door, and I'm really drooping here," she said, clasping his grandfather's hand between both of hers.

"I see what you are doing," the old man grumbled at Rey, "but for this young woman, I will do the gentlemanly thing and escort her home."

He slowly rose to his feet, slapping away at Rey's hand as he reached to support him.

"I'm not completely incapable yet."

He straightened to his full height and stared Rey straight in the eye. "You will tell me. The minute you hear anything."

"*Sí, Abuelo*. I promise."

Rey turned to Sara and took both her hands in his. "Go home, rest, I will call you when I hear anything."

"I'll be back in the morning," she promised, reaching up to kiss him lightly on the cheek.

It was a butterfly-light touch but every nerve in his body centered on that one spot. As she left the room with his grandfather and Javier, he pressed his fingers to the exact place her lips had touched.

"You've got it bad, *mi hermano*. If I hadn't seen it myself, I wouldn't have believed it. I was worried when you announced your engagement to us and implied you weren't serious about it. I'm pleased to see you were only joking." Alex's voice broke the brief spell that had captured him in its net.

Rey was momentarily lost for words. Of course he and Sara had kissed before, kissed but nothing more. The engagement was a smoke screen only. A ruse to keep *Abuelo* from getting even more upset about the three-hundred-year-old legend that had become his obsession.

At least that's all it was supposed to be. Maybe it was just the extreme situation they found themselves in with Benedict's accident, some age-old instinct to survive at all costs, but right now he wanted a whole lot more than kisses from Sara.

He pushed aside his reaction with a laugh. It was merely the tension of the situation—the worry over Benedict—and very probably, the length of time since he'd last taken a woman to his bed. It couldn't be anything more than that. Could it?

Three

Rina sat in the backseat of the sleek dark limousine next to the eldest del Castillo, yet her mind was filled with the image of her sister's fiancé. She fully understood the attraction. In fact, she was left fighting it herself.

It was all wrong. She and Sara had never been attracted to the same kind of guy before. Ever. While physically, both Rina and Sara's tastes had run to the tall, dark and handsome guys, Sara was all about presence. She fell for men with as much charisma as swagger. Rina's men had always been quiet achievers. The kind of guys who were strong and successful but not necessarily right up there on the podium announcing their achievements—the sort you might not look at twice, but if you did, you didn't regret it. Men like Jacob, although his quiet achievements hadn't exactly led them along the path she'd expected. Especially not when he'd told her the woman he now loved was his boss.

"It's the curse, you know," Aston del Castillo's voice interrupted her reverie.

"The curse?"

"I see he hasn't told you about it yet. Of course, he doesn't believe in it, but it's real."

Her curiosity piqued, Rina started to ask what the curse was, exactly, but instead the old man muttered something in Spanish and seemed to doze off.

Rina leaned forward and tapped Javier on the shoulder. "Is he okay? He just fell asleep."

She saw Javier's eyes in the rearview mirror and then a smile split his face. "*Sí*, the *señor* is fine. He is tired and refuses to admit he is not as strong as he used to be."

At the cottage, Javier saw her to the front door and waited until she was inside and had turned the iron key in the large black lock before returning to the car. Rina turned around and faced the main room, this time really seeing it properly.

Uneven beams ran the length of the cottage ceiling. Rather than being dark or daunting, the warmth of the wooden spines that gave the structure its strength was friendly and welcoming combined with the pale creamy apricot-tinted plaster between each. The low rays of the last of the evening sun speared in through the multipaned, deep-set windows. The simple wooden dining suite, and the chintz-covered sofas in the sitting room area, were clearly not new, but retained the patina of time and wear like badges of honor.

Shelves were built into a recess along one wall, and beneath them a modern television cabinet and stereo unit lounged side-by-side. Rina flicked on the TV, suddenly anxious to disperse the silence of being alone.

She dropped her bag onto the wooden tabletop and made her way through the open-plan living area to the small kitchen. A gas stove, with a shiny new chrome kettle on one of the burners caught her attention. She filled it and set it on the stove to boil. An old-fashioned coal range dominated the space beside the stove.

Her stomach growled as she opened the small refrigerator tucked in beneath the bench and was relieved to see her sister had left some food behind. Cheese, some slightly limp vegetables, eggs and a little leftover milk. The expiry date on the milk bottle suggested it was well overdue.

Rina's brow furrowed. Her sister could be erratic but she'd always been very particular about food safety after a serious bout of food poisoning when they were first flatting together in their late teens. It wasn't like Sara not to clean out perishables before going somewhere—she was a stickler for observing expiry dates. This whole situation just got more and more confusing. Had Sara first gone to France in a bit of a rush, expecting to return sooner than today? But then why would she have gone back again? Just trying to make sense of it was making Rina's head hurt.

Another rumble from the pit of her belly reminded her it had been a good eight or more hours since her last meal. As slender as she was, Rina had a high metabolism and usually ate regularly.

She grabbed the eggs and the best of all the vegetables from the fridge and whipped up a frittata for her supper. Tomorrow she'd have to find some way of gathering more groceries to replenish Sara's supply—especially if there would be the two of them here soon.

Rina had not long finished her meal and had cleaned up her dishes when she heard a car approach on the road to the cottage. She had the door open as the now familiar Ferrari pulled to a stop outside.

Her heart hammered in her chest as Reynard unfolded from the driver's seat and walked through the gate. The suit coat was gone, as well as the immaculately knotted rich burgundy silk tie he'd worn earlier in the day. With his face cast in relief by the setting sun, she couldn't make out his expression but weariness and dejection pulled at every line of his body. Each step was slow and deliberate. Rina felt unexpected tears prick at her eyes. Clearly the news about his brother was not good.

"Benedict? Is he going to be okay?" she asked softly as he reached the front porch.

"He's made it through surgery and he's in intensive care. Only one of us is allowed in at a time, and only for short periods. Alex and Loren will stay at the hospital tonight and I'll head in first thing in the morning."

His voice was flat, as if he couldn't believe the day his family had endured. Instantly, the urge to provide comfort flooded through Rina's veins. She opened her arms to him as he entered the cottage and without hesitation he clasped her to him.

He was lean muscle from top to toe, and fraught with a tension that held his body tight like a bow.

"He'll be all right, Rey," she murmured into the broad warmth of his shoulder.

"They've done everything they can—now it's up to him."

His voice was a guttural whisper. Rina was rocked by the strength of emotion she felt pouring from him. The three brothers had to be close, judging by how distraught he was. She couldn't even begin to imagine what they were all going through. She struggled to find the words that might provide him with some comfort.

"He's young and he's strong, and with you and Alex there for him, he'll pull through."

"I don't know what I'll do if he doesn't."

Rina closed her eyes against the building moisture there.

The fear in Rey's voice struck her to her core. She knew if it was Sara there in the ICU, she'd be frantic with worry herself. Slowly she edged from his embrace and pulled away to close the front door.

"Come in, I'll make you a warm drink—unless you'd like something stronger?"

"No, coffee will be fine. I want to have my wits about me should Alex call."

Rina nodded and went through to the kitchen and busied herself measuring coffee for the old-fashioned stovetop percolator she'd found in a cupboard earlier in the evening. She sent a silent prayer of thanks skyward that Sara had thought to include in her letter that Reynard took his coffee black and sweet. In her peripheral vision she saw Rey drop into one of the fabric covered sofas, his tall frame all but dwarfing the feminine piece of furniture. He leaned forward and rested his elbows on his knees, rubbing at his eyes with long, tanned fingers.

Once the coffee had percolated, she poured it into a mug and placed it, a spoon and a sugar bowl on a small tray and carried it to Rey.

"Thanks," he said, taking the mug off the tray and dropping two cubes of sugar into the steaming liquid and stirred—the clink of the spoon against the ceramic mug loud in the quiet of the room.

Rina settled onto the facing sofa and watched as he drained the mug in a series of slow pulls. "More?" she asked as he put the mug down on the coffee table between them.

"No, thanks. I suppose I should head back into town, to my place." He gave a massive yawn. "Sooner, rather than later."

"You could stay here," Rina offered, even though she had no idea if the cottage boasted more than one bedroom.

An unsettling thought occurred to her. Wouldn't he expect to sleep in the same bed with her? What if he wanted to be intimate—to seek comfort from the shock of his brother's near death in her arms? He was her sister's fiancé—wouldn't that be normal under the circumstances? What on earth had she been thinking inviting him to stay?

Rey shot her a heavy-lidded look. "Are you sure?"

Oh God, what had she done? She could always plead a headache, a period, or tiredness herself, she supposed. But what if this ridiculous attraction she felt for him enticed her into doing something she knew she shouldn't?

Reason overcame fear. He was shattered, and she knew firsthand the physical toll emotional exhaustion took on a person. She doubted he'd have the energy to do anything more than hold her while she slept. A prospect that she had to admit, she found almost too appealing. But it wouldn't go beyond that. Above all, he was her sister's fiancé—she could never betray Sara's trust like that. Ever.

"Hey, I think one del Castillo in the hospital right now is enough, don't you?"

He smiled a sweet, crooked smile. "Two, if you count *Abuelo* at the convalescent home."

"Good point," she agreed with a smile. "They say three's a charm but let's not tempt fate, shall we?"

"I'll get my things from the car."

His things? Did he often sleep over?

"I always keep a set ready in case I stay with one of my brothers," he explained, in response to the obvious surprise on her face.

"I'll, um…I'll go use the bathroom while you settle in, then."

Rina bolted for the bedroom and shoved her suitcase in a small closet, then rifled through her sister's chest of drawers for a nightgown, praying she still possessed at least one or two that were halfway decent. If he had slept here before, he'd know about things like that, wouldn't he?

She fervently wished, not for the first time today, that Sara hadn't put her in this position. Her fingers closed around an old, oversize T-shirt. She lifted it from the drawer and shook it out. Should be long enough, she surmised—and not sexy enough, which was even more important. Rina bunched the fabric in one fist and made it to the bathroom even as she heard Rey come back in through the front door.

The old metal lock clicked into place, the sound echoing through the tiny cottage like a knell of some sort. She swallowed against the sudden knot of tension that lodged in the base of her throat. What she wouldn't give for a chance to talk to Sara right this minute.

She swung the bathroom door shut behind her and reached for the toiletries she'd scattered around the bathroom before her shower. It only took a couple of minutes to wash her face free of makeup and brush her hair. She took her time over her teeth, even as she promised herself it didn't make any difference. It wasn't as if she and Reynard del Castillo would be indulging in anything other than sleep tonight.

By the time she pulled the soft, worn T-shirt over her head, her heart was beating erratically. If she didn't get a hold of herself soon she'd be the next one in hospital. Rina forced herself to breathe slowly; her fingers curled tight around the cool, white porcelain pedestal basin as if it was her only anchor in the world. She could do this. All she had to do was fall asleep. Should be simple, right? Forget that the time at home was something ridiculous like seven or eight in the morning—her body clock was so out of whack she should be on the verge of falling asleep on her feet.

But instead all she could think about was how it had felt to be pressed hard up against the strength of Reynard's body. How his scent had filled her nostrils. Not just the scent of the male fragrance he wore, but *him*. The man exuded pheromones, if her body's reaction was any judge. Any poor judge, she reminded herself. But the desperate truth was that she craved to be held like that again—to be made to feel precious and treasured. Safe. Wanted.

She blinked and slowly peeled her fingers from the basin. He'd be waiting to use the bathroom by now. She forced herself to turn and pick up her clothes from the tiled floor and open the door.

In the bedroom Reynard sat quietly on the edge of the bed, a small, black leather toilet bag between his hands. He looked up as she entered.

"Are you sure you're all right with this?" he asked.

"Of course I am," Rina breezed, with what she hoped was the right amount of savoir faire.

"I won't be long," he replied, rising from the bed and heading for the bathroom. "I can sleep on the sofa if you'd rather."

"As if you'd fit." Rina forced a smile. "Don't be silly. It's fine, really."

Rey gave a short nod and went through to the bathroom and closed the door. Rina scuttled under the crisp white sheets on the bed and inhaled the faint scent of lavender. Maybe he'd take his time. Maybe she'd even be asleep before he got into bed with her.

She lay facing the edge of the bed, closed her eyes and tried to let her head sink into the pillow, but every tense muscle in her body had other ideas and she felt as if she was rigidly surfing on top of the scented cotton. By the time she heard Reynard come back into the bedroom, switch off the bedside lamp and felt the mattress depress under the weight of his body, she could barely breathe again.

"This isn't how I imagined we'd spend our first night together," Reynard's voice murmured from close behind her.

Their *first* night together? It was true in more ways than he knew. Rina mumbled something indistinct in response. Beneath the sheets she could already feel the heat of his body only inches from hers. He shifted and she felt the weight of his arm over the top of the sheets and the thin bed cover as it draped across her body. The muscles in his arm bunched as he drew her up against his length. His bare chest seared through the thin cotton of her shirt and she felt his warm breath against the exposed skin of her shoulder.

"Sleep well," he said softly. "And thank you. It's good not to be alone with my fears tonight."

Rina remained silent. Sleep well? It was ironic. The last thing she wanted right now was sleep. His body, curled around hers, felt so right, yet everything about this was so very wrong. She listened carefully, her eyes burning in the darkened room. Soon his breathing settled into a deeper rhythm. His body relaxed against hers.

In the distance she could hear the sea. It was as if each breath from Rey's lungs matched the slow susurration of the waves as they caressed the coastline. Inch by slow inch she felt her body begin to relax, felt her own breathing slide into the gentle flow of the tide and the man behind her.

Rey knew the exact instant Sara accepted his presence behind her and slid into sleep. Her soft curves nestled against the planes of his body. It felt good to hold her, too good, he acknowledged as a certain part of his body showed no immediate signs of wanting to rest. He reminded himself why he was here—of the circumstances that had led to him being in Sara's bed tonight. It was as effective as a bucket of ice in his lap.

The memory of Benedict in that hospital bed, tubes and pipes snaking out from his body to various machines and apparatus—the knowledge that without them he wouldn't even be breathing on his own—was almost more than he could bear.

Rey's arm tightened around Sara's sleeping form and she instinctively snuggled closer against him, her neatly curved buttocks firm against his groin.

Dios, under any other circumstances he'd delight in waking her again. In losing himself, and the events of today, in the softness of her feminine curves. In spite of his plans to keep their relationship platonic to ease the sting when it ended, there was no denying that for the time being, they were engaged, even if it was mostly just for show. They were still a pair of normal healthy adults with normal healthy appetites.

But a del Castillo had more honor than that, he reminded himself. He'd been relieved at Sara's old-fashioned attitudes—allowing no more than a few kisses, a little light petting—because they'd given him the comfort of knowing that when they went their separate ways, there would be no serious heartbreak or recriminations. Tonight, however, he'd needed to hold her in his arms, and the realization shocked him on a new level. He hadn't expected to need her.

She seemed different today, he thought, even taking into account that the circumstances were completely out of sync with their normal lives. He couldn't quite put his finger on what it was. It was more than the coffee she'd drunk at the hospital, when he hadn't seen her drink the beverage since before she went to France. There was a sense of calm about her that was at odds with the party girl he'd first been attracted to.

Sure, he knew she could be focused. The accolades she'd earned on the dressage and other equestrian event circuits were mute proof of that. But her attitude today had been more. It was something that went beyond the superficial, something that spoke to him, instead, on a deeper level. A level that drew him to her for the comfort he now hungered for. How had that happened in the space of a few hours when before he'd had no difficulty keeping his emotional distance?

Whatever it was, he acceded—as sleep finally drew him under and he lost himself in the soft and slightly unfamiliar fragrance of Sara's hair as it streamed over her pillow—she had been exactly what he'd needed today.

Four

Reynard woke as sunshine streamed through the unshuttered windows. For a moment he was disoriented—both by the furnishings around him and the warm, lithe body sprawled across his. One part of his body, however, suffered no such disorientation.

In fact, that particular part of his body was creating undue influence on the state of his mind, particularly with the soft scent of Sara's hair filling his nostrils and the exposed creamy skin of her legs entangled with his.

She'd lost some of her light golden tan, he noticed. He fought the urge to stroke his hand over the delicious length of thigh exposed by her nightshirt riding up over the gentle round globes of her buttocks. And a little weight, too, he'd wager. What on earth had she been up to while she was away?

Reynard closed his eyes and breathed in a slow, steady breath—but even as he did so, the blend of fragrance from her hair and the feminine scent of her skin intoxicated him, stirring his body even more. His eyes flashed open again. The deprivation of that sensory input had only served to sharpen everything else. Painfully so, if his current condition was any indicator.

He let his eyes wander over her slumbering form again. Whatever the changes in Sara, he couldn't help but enjoy a certain voyeuristic pleasure in taking an eyeful while she still slept. Their open-ended engagement hadn't covered morning talk, or morning anything, for that matter, until now. Perhaps it would be worth exploring things a little further by coaxing her awake the most pleasurable way he knew how.

The discreet chirp of his cell phone in the main room of the cottage was a stark reminder to keep himself in check. There were more serious considerations in his life right now than whether or not Sara tasted as good as she smelled.

He eased his body out from under hers, freezing for a moment as she muttered something in her sleep and then repositioned herself on the pillow he'd used. There were still purple shadows under her eyes and her face was still as pale as she'd been ever since the previous afternoon when she'd come to his office. Whatever she'd been doing recently, it hadn't been restful, that much was certain. He adjusted his boxers and slipped from the room to answer his phone.

The news about Benedict, while not brilliant, was hopeful and it was time he relieved Alex and Loren in their vigil. He quickly showered and dressed into the change of clothes he'd brought last night and left a brief note explaining where he'd gone on the kitchen countertop.

She was still sleeping when he returned to the bedroom—he hadn't been quite able to resist one last glance before he headed to the hospital. She'd moved again, and beneath the sheet he could see her foot stroking back and forth—a tiny movement, even as she slept—across the sheets. So she was a sensualist, he surmised, feeling the tight knot that hadn't quite left him intensify low in his gut. Texture, sensation—he really had to stop torturing himself but he couldn't tear his gaze away.

The edge of her shirt now rode even higher on those long slender legs, exposing the gentlest hint of the curve of her buttocks as she lay half-sprawled on her stomach, one arm pushed far under the pillow. The fabric of the top was thin, and pulled tight under her arm and across the swell of one breast.

Even as he watched, she shifted again. Rolling onto her back. His mouth dried. She was like a ripe peach. Her dark red hair spread in spiraling disarray around her face. Her eyelids flickered—no doubt she'd be awake soon. He debated crossing the short distance to the bed and placing a fleeting kiss on the lush pale pink width of her lips. Just the thought of doing so was enough to make his fingers tighten on the brass handle of the bedroom door.

He shook his head slightly. Rey quickly drew the bedroom door closed with a faint "snick" of sound. How did she do that, all of a sudden? How did she make him forget so quickly, so effortlessly, when before it had been she who had so easily blurred from his thoughts?

Rina stretched against the cotton sheets and yawned—then sat bolt upright. Reynard? Where was he? She grabbed at the hem of her nightshirt and pulled it down hard, then, realizing how it stretched the material against her upper body, let it go again. She slipped from the bed and to the bedroom door, listening carefully for sounds of movement. Nothing.

Cautiously, she opened the door and listened again. While the noise of birds chattering wildly filtered through from outside, the cottage merely reflected an echo of emptiness.

Muscles she didn't even know she'd tensed, eased as she realized he really was gone. She didn't know just how well she'd have been able to keep up the charade. Which reminded her, she needed to get a hold of Sara and find out exactly when she planned to be back.

Rina found her BlackBerry and dialed her sister's number. A frown pulled at her eyebrows as the call went straight through to voice mail. For a second she was tempted to hang up and just try again and again until Sara eventually answered, but she tempered that with the knowledge that her sister had never willingly and actively avoided her before, so she left a message.

"There's been an accident. Benedict's hurt. I'm sure they're expecting me—or rather, *you*—at the hospital again today and I don't know how long I can fake this. Please call me, Sara. Please?"

With an exasperated sigh she ended the call and walked across the cool tiled floor to the kitchen. On the bench she saw Rey's note. Her eyes skimmed the words, written in a bold, slashing script. So he'd send a car for her about ten, would he? She looked at the wall clock above the kitchen stove. That gave her about two hours to get ready. And two hours to figure out how to tell him the truth about Sara. The prospect settled in her stomach like congealed oatmeal—heavy and completely unappetizing.

Rina gathered a set of fresh clothes and went to shower and get dressed. With any luck, she'd make it to the nearest town to get some much-needed groceries, and back, before facing Rey again for what, depending on his reaction, might be the last time ever.

* * *

The huge black bicycle, with a basket attached to the front, had Rina scratching her head for a few moments. Dare she risk it? There was no helmet, no chain guard, not even a set of gears on the thing—and judging by the cobwebs draping the frame it hadn't moved past the lean-to shelter at the back of the cottage in some time.

She shuddered. She hated spiders. But as much as she hated spiders, she liked eating more, and her light breakfast had pretty much taken care of the remainder of the perishables in the house. She picked up a twig from a pile of kindling that was stacked just inside the lean-to, next to a larger pile of split wood, and carefully removed the spider webs before rolling the behemoth out into the sunlight and checking the tires.

The old bicycle pump, set on a bracket on the cross beam of the bike, thankfully lived up to its designated task of filling the tires with much-needed air. She cocked her head and listened. No telltale hiss anywhere. Deciding to err on the side of caution, Rina did a few short circuits up and down the road outside the cottage. Satisfied that the tires would hold, she gathered her wallet from inside, and the key, and popped them in the basket before rolling up the hem of her cotton trousers. Maybe white wasn't quite the best choice, she thought as she straddled the bike and wobbled her way up the road.

She'd been pedaling for no more than a couple of kilometers when a dust cloud approached her from the distance. Since she'd figured out this was a private road, she was surprised to see another vehicle coming her way. And quickly, too, if the smear of dust particles in the air was any indicator.

As the vehicle drew closer, she recognized Reynard's Ferrari. He slowed down and wheeled to a halt in the dirt road. Rina waited a moment for the dust to settle before getting closer.

His window rolled down and he leaned one arm along the open frame.

"What on earth are you doing?" he asked.

Rina bristled. It didn't take a rocket scientist to figure it out, surely.

"I'm riding a bike. I need some supplies."

"Since when did you ride a bike to get them?" he commented as he thrust open his door and unfolded his length from the car.

Her eyes drank in the sight of him. He was dressed in pale gray trousers, teamed with a long-sleeved, lightweight white knit sweater, with the sleeves pushed up to expose tanned muscled forearms with a light sprinkling of dark hair. His hazel eyes were obscured by a dark pair of designer sunglasses and his hair was swept off his forehead by the light breeze. Altogether he was a mouthwatering sight.

Realizing he was standing there waiting for an answer, she scoured her memory for what he'd just said and grabbed at the first thought that sprang to mind.

"I'm running out of a few things."

"So why didn't you just do as you always do and leave a list for the cleaner?"

Rina stifled a groan and mentally shook a fist at her sister for neatly landing her in it. She felt as if she had to walk on eggshells from here on in.

"I needed the exercise," she explained with a shrug. "Besides, it's a lovely morning and I wasn't expecting you for a while yet. How's Benedict today?"

"The doctors are talking about bringing him out of the induced coma today. *Abuelo* and Javier are at the hospital now so I thought I'd come and collect you early."

"Right, well, you'd better follow me, then," Rina suggested as she turned the bike around and hopped up on the worn saddle.

"Or we could just leave the bike here, and collect it when we come back," Rey said with one eyebrow quirked as if all his humor at the sight on her on the bike was hidden behind those dark lenses of his.

"No, I couldn't do that. It might get stolen. What would the owners say?"

"Sara, stop pulling my leg. I am the owner—of the cottage and everything in it. Or at least my family is, anyway. You know that."

Rina suddenly put it all together. The beautiful golden castillo she'd seen through the kitchen window by the cliff tops only a mile or two away. Reynard's surname. That whole sense of entitlement and privilege that she'd sensed about him and his brother from the minute she'd laid eyes on them. That also explained why Sara was staying at the Governess's Cottage. It was a family property; where else would one's fiancée stay if they weren't actually staying with you?

"Well, I'd still rather put it away. Don't want to get on the wrong side of you or anything," she half joked.

The tiny pull at the corner of his lips sent a zing straight to her chest. Serious faced, he was handsome as sin, but with that quirky little half smile he was devastating. She began to pedal, hoping that she wouldn't do anything stupid like wobble right off the road and into a ditch. She heard the slow purr of his car's engine as he cruised along behind at a snail's pace.

Every time her feet depressed the pedals she was conscious of how her backside must look to him. Of how the cotton pants she wore stretched tight across her buttocks and thighs. By the time she reached the cottage she was hot and flustered. Noticing that she'd smeared some chain grease on her pants leg, despite her efforts to the contrary, she excused herself to change before they left for the hospital.

Eschewing her own suitcase, she thrust open the doors to Sara's wardrobe and grabbed the first thing she found on a hanger. The fact it was a light floral dress with a background of mint green and a designer label on it that shrieked a budget far higher than Rina usually allowed herself for clothing was merely a side benefit, she decided as she yanked off her shirt and trousers and then shimmied into the dress. Sara always did prefer to spend her money rather than sock it away for a rainy day, and for once, Rina wholeheartedly approved.

She knew Sara wouldn't begrudge Rina borrowing her clothes, had in fact even suggested it, but Rina had the feeling this particular dress was special. It certainly felt that way as the deliciously soft fabric whispered across her legs as she slid her feet into a pair of matching open toe pumps.

She quickly stepped into the bathroom to freshen her makeup and to check her phone surreptitiously. At last! A text from Sara. Rina groaned under her breath in frustration. Was it too much to ask for her runaway sister to have finally responded at a time when Rina could call or text her back? Rina scanned the message.

Sori I hvn't been in touch. I hope things r ok with Ben. Pls, whateva u do, don't tell Rey wot I've done. Will call u soon. Luv u sis. Sx

Rina's heart sank. She'd geared herself up to give Reynard the full story and now here was Sara once more begging her not to. It made her sick to her stomach but despite her own feelings on the matter she decided to give Sara that little extra leeway. With any luck, she'd be back in a day or so and everything would be fine.

Reluctantly, she switched the phone to silent mode. If Sara called now she'd have to go to voice mail. Rina sincerely doubted she'd be able to carry off a phone conversation with her twin while said twin's fiancé sat next to her in the close confines of his car. And, of course, the hospital expected cell phones to be switched off in the high dependency unit where Benedict was currently being cared for. Rina remembered that much at least from when their father had suffered his last, fatal heart attack.

"Sara? Are you ready? We really need to get back now."

Rey's voice outside the bathroom door made her start. She turned on a faucet and let cool water splash over her wrists for a second before snapping it off.

"Just a minute. I'm nearly done," she called over her shoulder.

She grabbed her perfume and spritzed a tiny amount behind each ear before grabbing the length of her hair and twisting it up into a loose knot secured with a handful of Sara's pins. There was one advantage in having the same untamed mass of long red hair—they both tended to wear it in very similar styles. There. She could handle anything, she decided as she looked at herself in the mirror. Anything that didn't get too personal, at least.

As they left the cottage she heard Rey inhale softly.

"Nice perfume. It's different from your usual."

Rina swallowed against the gasp of irritation that rose in her throat. She hadn't even thought about what perfume Sara had been wearing. Her sister had always preferred the spicier floral, oriental-based perfumes while she herself was more a light floral fragrance person. It was yet another example of how careful she was going to have to be to carry this off properly.

She turned and smiled at Rey, slipping on a pair of sunglasses so he couldn't see the lie in her eyes. Sara always warned her that she gave too much away.

"It's something I picked up while I was away. Do you like it?"

From behind her, Rey leaned in and inhaled again, his lips mere centimeters from the curve of her neck.

"Mmm, yeah, I do."

A frisson of awareness shot down Rina's spine with the velocity of lightning, leaving a fierce sizzle throbbing in its wake. She stumbled a little, steadying as Rey's hands shot out to anchor her.

"I'm okay," she hastened to say, pulling from his light clasp before she could enjoy getting too close.

What was it she had told herself only minutes ago? About handling things provided it didn't get too personal? Right now, it looked as if that was to be her biggest obstacle because despite everything, she was left fighting against a desire to get very personal indeed.

Five

The updated news at the hospital wasn't good. Rather than attempt to bring Benedict out of his coma, Rey was shocked to learn the doctors had reassessed his condition and elected to keep him in that suspended state for at least two more days. While his air bags had deployed and saved him from more serious head injuries, there was still some swelling on the brain that was causing concern. Another forty-eight excruciating hours of hoping against hope their brother would find the will to fight his way out of the pain and darkness, and survive.

Rey leaned back on the hard, vinyl-covered seat in the private waiting room and exchanged a look with Alex. Somehow they had to get through this—more importantly, somehow they had to get *Benedict* through this. Rey didn't need words to know that he and Alex were remembering their last evening with the three of them together.

It had been weeks ago, the night of *Abuelo*'s stroke, and

they'd all gathered at the castillo for dinner together. Rey had announced his engagement to Sara to his brothers, and Ben had seen right through his plans. Despite the agreement they'd made three and a half months prior, to find brides to calm *Abuelo*'s fears, Benedict knew Rey had no intention of seeing the engagement through to marriage. *Abuelo*'s constant harping about the governess's curse was making him ill and had caused huge concern among the brothers—so much so, it had forced Alex to go ahead with the archaic arranged marriage he'd never planned to take seriously, and both Rey and Benedict to agree to do whatever it took to keep *Abuelo* well and happy.

The fact that Alex's marriage to Loren had turned out to be a whole lot happier than anyone had anticipated was beside the point. It certainly had come close to failing completely because of his brother's pride and stubbornness—a pride and stubbornness that was bred in all the del Castillo men, it would seem.

Rey felt a cold trickle of unease creep under his skin. Perhaps his grandfather had been right. Perhaps the curse really was coming full circle and Benedict's accident had been yet another reminder that the surviving del Castillo sons had to abide by honor, truth and love with their whole hearts in order to keep the family alive for another generation. His rational side rejected the thought emphatically, but who knew now how much truth there remained in the legendary curse, especially given the problems Alex and Loren had originally faced in their marriage, *Abuelo*'s stroke and now Benedict's life-threatening injuries?

Could the crazed words of a scorned woman really have such an effect nine generations later—with theirs reputed to be the last if they didn't get their act together? Again, that finger of disquiet stroked a chilling line down his neck. He huffed a sigh in frustration and shifted again on his chair. All this inactivity made him uncomfortable. It left him too much time to think.

The doctors only permitted one family member in with Benedict at a time, and only for about ten minutes each hour, at that. Loren had just returned from being with him now and Rey recognized the shell-shocked expression on her face as mirroring his own after his visit with Ben. He had found it both terrifying and frustrating to see his younger sibling so pale and bruised, his body covered with dressings over wounds, tubes and wires coming out everywhere—even a machine that aided his breathing.

Neither he nor Alex felt they could leave the hospital after this morning's news. Benedict's condition was too fragile. They had to remain, even if they couldn't be in the same room with their injured brother, they just had to be *here*. Their sentiments were strongly echoed by *Abuelo* who had stubbornly fought to stay at the hospital all day also, but whose exhaustion had finally seen him reluctantly agree to return to his room in the convalescent home for some much needed rest.

Rey shifted again on the seat. *Dios,* they were so uncomfortable. No wonder the old man tired so quickly. And where the hell had Sara gone? She'd left him a couple of hours ago, with Javier and *Abuelo*, on the pretext of "sorting some things out." Just what did she have to sort out, he wondered irritably. Her place was at his side—or at least to be seen at his side.

Now she was back from France, he was even more firmly reminded of the need to portray to his family that he was following the terms all the brothers had agreed upon. That they'd do whatever it took to give their grandfather the peace of mind he needed to stop worrying about the blasted curse. Well, he was doing his part, together with

Sara. Now it was up to Benedict to get well and do the very same.

A sound at the door to the waiting room caught his attention and he and Alex exchanged a puzzled look before they both rose to their feet to see what the commotion was about. If it kept up, then soon the charge nurse on the floor would be along, exhorting them to be quiet with her usual quelling glare. To Rey's surprise the door opened to reveal a crew of maintenance staff with large trolleys—one empty and the others stacked with covered, bulky loads. The men came into the room, closely followed by Sara who had a very smug smile on her face.

"Thank you, gentlemen. Yes, these are the ones to go and then you can bring in the new furniture."

"New furniture?" Rey asked, looking askance at his fiancée. What on earth was she thinking? New furniture in a hospital waiting room?

"Yes," she said, stepping out of the way of the two men as they stacked up the vinyl-coated chairs and loaded them onto the empty trolley before bringing in a very comfortable-looking three-seater sofa and two recliners, together with a set of highly polished side tables and a small credenza. "New furniture. No one can possibly be comfortable on those things." She gestured to the trolley outside the door. "Besides, if I'd only gotten the one recliner for *Abuelo* he would have refused to use it, wouldn't he?"

There was no argument there. The old man would have sat on the floor rather than admit that his age and infirmity granted him the privilege of a more comfortable seat than anyone else.

"Of course, you are right," Rey acknowledged, side-stepping one of the maintenance crew who was positioning the credenza against a wall near a power socket. "He most definitely would have refused it."

It was astute of Sara to have picked up that so quickly— she'd only met the del Castillo patriarch yesterday—astute and caring of an old man's need for comfort. Rey gave her a narrowed glance. Since when did she get so perceptive? When she smiled back in response, he felt an unexpected rush of something new toward Sara, something warm and heart deep. The sensation took him by surprise and made him a little uncomfortable at the same time. He was unused to feeling this way about a woman. Usually he indulged in what became a mutually satisfying physical affair. He always played all the right moves to ensure that each of his companions were made to feel special and treasured for however long he planned to spend with them. With Sara it had been no different, until she'd returned from France, that is.

It was as if she was two different people, or as if the Sara he'd asked to become his fiancée, carefully couching the proposal as "let's get engaged" so there was no actual mention of marriage, had changed while she'd been away. The differences were both disconcerting and appealing at the same time.

It was because of Benedict's accident, he told himself. It couldn't possibly be anything else. She hadn't changed, it was just his perception of her that was different, given his state of mind. His emotions were all over the place at the thought that one of his beloved brothers, no matter their occasional differences, could be lost to them.

But even as he tried to convince himself of this, he couldn't help asking himself whether the Sara he'd known before would have thought so far ahead to an elderly man's comfort, not to mention his pride, let alone to have conjured up an espresso machine together with a small refrigerator to store fresh, healthy snacks and milk for all the family.

Maybe he'd misjudged her. Even as he thought of it, the notion refused to make sense. Reynard trusted his people sense. It was an indispensable business skill that he'd spent years developing. He knew what Sara was like—had known ever since he'd met her at the annual del Castillo–sponsored equestrian trials. But how could one woman be so completely different? On the one hand, the life of the party—fun and flirtatious—then on the other, kind and compassionate and imbued with a warmth that went straight to people's hearts. It wasn't logical. The Sara he knew was taking her responsibility to him and his family far more seriously than he'd ever intended. Now, he was starting to believe that she was hardly the type to simply laugh and brush off a broken engagement, either. While he had no desire to actually marry her, a sudden protective surge warned him that he had no desire to hurt her, either.

What if he really married her, a little voice asked from deep inside. No, he quelled the thought immediately. That wasn't part of the plan. He didn't believe in the curse so it shouldn't matter whether he was engaged or married, or anything for that matter. He'd never given the state of marriage a great deal of thought—it was just something he knew would happen "one day"—but he did know that when he finally embarked on such a course, he'd be doing it because *he* was ready, not at the behest of a frightened old man, no matter how much he loved his grandfather. Despite his inner demons he had to acknowledge that he had begun to crave Sara in ways he'd never done before.

He reached for her, noting briefly the expression of surprise that danced across her beautiful face, and drew her into his arms. She held herself stiffly for a moment, before her body melted against his. Soft against hard. Feminine against the masculine. And it felt right. Shockingly, amazingly right. Every part of his body attuned to hers. His breathing slowed and steadied and it was almost as if his heart now beat to the same rhythm as that of the woman in his arms. For the first time in hours, he actually relaxed.

"Thank you," he murmured against the top of her fiery head. "You have been amazing."

"I aim to please," she said teasingly, clearly trying to make light of the situation. "Besides, I only arranged a short-term lease on the items, but I thought your family might like to make the furnishings a permanent donation to the hospital for other families that are going through what you guys are."

She pulled free of his arms and walked over to the coffee machine, and picked up the instruction booklet. Even though she made a show of reading it, he could tell their brief contact had unsettled her. Unsettled *her?* It had totally unsettled *him,* as well. His blood pumped with a new demand through his veins. His senses were totally in sync with her and her alone. Not even Loren and Alex's quiet appreciation of the new furniture, as they cuddled at one end of the couch totally lost in one another, broke through the focus that was Sara's and hers alone.

Rina felt the hairs on the back of her neck prickle under Rey's sharp regard. It had been all too easy to flow into his arms just then. She hadn't wanted to pull away but had forced herself to do so before she became altogether too comfortable. She kept reminding herself this was only temporary and that once the crisis with Benedict had passed, and she fervently hoped it would, she'd be able to tell Reynard the truth about why she was here instead of her sister.

A part of her wished she hadn't agreed to Sara's plans. Or that she'd insisted on telling Reynard the truth the moment she'd met him at his office. But seeing what all the members of the family were going through, she couldn't do that to him, as well. She knew firsthand how it felt to be rejected by the person you'd promised to marry. How much worse would it be if that happened while another person you loved fought for their life at the same time?

No, what she'd do instead was what she did best and what she made her living doing as a contract "Girl Friday" back home. Already, her knowledge and experience in publicity and problem solving was standing her in good stead in her self-appointed mission to make sure the family was taken care of as they dealt with Benedict's crisis. She'd make certain that every aspect of the del Castillos' time at the hospital went as smoothly as possible so they could focus on the person who needed them most. Whether it was organizing nutritious meals to be brought to their waiting room, or changes of clothes and access to a shower and bathroom, she'd make it happen.

And the truth? Well, she'd face up to that as soon as she could. As unpalatable as that would be.

The next two days passed painfully slowly. The family appeared to be trapped in a fugue of uncertainty until finally, at midday on the third day, Benedict's doctor came to the waiting room. Rina was almost too afraid to hope for good news as the man entered, his face looked so severe. But then, to everyone's great relief, a smile spread across his features.

"Señor del Castillo has made great progress in the past two days. He is coming out of the induced coma and all the indicators are looking strong at this stage. Of course, his full recovery will be demanding, but I am sure that with the support of his family, he will make it."

Rey and Alex peppered the doctor with questions after that but Rina noticed that *Abuelo* remained in his chair, his eyes suddenly awash with tears. She dropped to her knees and took his gnarled hands in her own.

"It's good news, *Abuelo*. Benedict will be all right. He's strong, he will make it."

Aston del Castillo lifted a hand to stroke her hair gently. "Thank you, I know he will survive. He is a del Castillo. Now we must fight the curse before it is too late."

Rina had overheard mutterings of the curse before but still no one had told her exactly what was involved.

"Too late?" she asked. "Tell me, why would it be too late?"

"They are running out of time. They refuse to believe it. Even Reynard." The old man shook his head slowly before fixing her with a slightly manic stare. "But you can make it work. You can help break the curse. She will not wait forever."

"*Señor,* you mustn't worry the *señorita* so," Javier interrupted before Aston could say anymore. "Thank you, Mees Woodville, you have made our vigil here so much more comfortable for two old men."

"Pah, old men. Speak for yourself," Aston said with a chuckle to his manservant.

Rina slowly rose to her feet. She wouldn't hear any more from *Abuelo* about the curse today, and now with Benedict's improvement and the promise he'd be out of intensive care in the next day or two, she knew they probably didn't need her here quite as much as they had. She was happy for Benedict—happy for all the del Castillo family—but suddenly it made facing reality just that much harder.

After the doctor had left and everyone had agreed to head to their respective homes for a break before taking shifts to return in the evening, Rina went up to Rey and lightly touched him on the arm.

"I'll go back to the cottage now. See you later, perhaps?"

"Let me drive you home," Reynard said smoothly, coming forward to take her by the hand.

"No, that's okay, I'm used to taking the taxi."

"And you shouldn't be. You're my fiancée and I should have been taking better care of you instead of the other way around. Thank you for all you've done."

"You're welcome, Rey, but seriously, it's what I do b—" She faltered before continuing. "It's what I'd do for anyone in this situation. You needed to keep your focus on Benedict."

For a minute she thought he'd press her on what she'd been about to say before she'd corrected herself, but thankfully he didn't. Instead, they made their goodbyes to the family and Javier before Rey led her out into the corridor, his fingers still lightly clasping her hand.

The contact sent a steady buzz of warmth up her arm. She still couldn't quite get used to this intensity of reaction every time he touched her. It wasn't normal, she was sure. Even with Jacob, whom she'd loved—still loved, she reminded herself sharply—she hadn't felt this tingling sense of attraction every single time their skin met.

The drive back to the cottage went swiftly. It was as if now that the pressure of worrying if Benedict would live or die had passed, Rey was in an all-fired hurry to resume his normal life. As they pulled up outside the cottage, Rina turned to him to thank him for the ride home but he was already getting out of the car and coming around to her door to open it for her.

"Thank you," she said, as he held the door and offered his hand to help her.

As he did, she noticed his eyes narrow, and his thumb stroked along her ring finger, particularly across the slightly paler band of skin there.

"Where is your ring?" he asked. "Why aren't you wearing it?"

Oh hell, she thought frantically. She hadn't stopped to think about the envelope Sara had given her on the day she'd arrived, or its obscenely valuable contents.

"I…I, um, I took it off the other night when I came back. I didn't want to get it dirty when I did the dishes and with everything that's been going on, I forgot to put it back on."

She fished in her bag and took out the key to the cottage, before swiftly inserting it in the ancient lock and pushing the door open. A few short steps took her to the table where she'd left Sara's envelope. She cursed herself for her stupidity. Rey could have seen it at any time and wondered what it was there for, and who this "Rina Woodville" was that it had been addressed to. And what if he'd read Sara's note?

She tipped the envelope and the ostentatious diamond solitaire fell into her hand. She slid the ring onto her finger, the cool metal a chilling brand against her skin and a reminder of the lie she'd agreed to perpetuate.

"There, see? Back where it belongs."

She smiled but to her surprise Reynard did not smile back. Oh Lord, had he guessed the truth? Did he realize now, for some reason, that she was not Sara?

Reynard looked at the ring upon Sara's finger and at the envelope from which she'd taken it, which still lay on the table. He'd only caught a glimpse of the front of the envelope, but that had been enough to see that it had her handwriting on it. Had she been on the verge of breaking things off with him? he wondered. Why else would she have put her ring in an envelope? An envelope that even now she was scrunching in the fist of one hand. Had it been addressed to him?

He couldn't let her do it. He couldn't let her back out. Especially not now. Aside from what it would do to *Abuelo*, he suddenly realized that he wasn't ready to let her go. If he was going to keep this working for as long as he needed, it was time to pull out all the stops. His responsibility to his family to project a united facade together with his brothers was primary. There was no room for second thoughts. The hell with keeping things platonic—if it took seducing her to make her stay then he'd do it.

So what if doing so was no great hardship. Rey closed his eyes for a second, refusing to admit, even to himself, that the prospect of seducing Sara held more allure than he wanted to acknowledge. He was doing this for his family.

"Would you like some coffee before you head home?" she said, although her voice sounded strained, as if what she really wanted was for him just to leave.

Well, he wasn't having that. Oh no. No one withdrew from Reynard del Castillo without his permission. Keeping his suspicions locked deep inside, Rey took a step toward her and was surprised to see her back away in response. He smiled. She could run, but she couldn't hide—not now he'd made up his mind about just what direction this engagement of theirs was to turn to next.

"No, thank you. I do not want coffee."

He deliberately let his gaze drop from her eyes to her lips, where he saw the tip of her tongue suddenly dart out to moisten their lush surface, before letting his view drop farther to her breasts. Her chest rose and fell quickly, betraying her nerves as he took another slow careful step toward her. He could see the outline of her nipples as they pressed against her softly patterned dress. Small sharp distended points begging for his touch.

"Something else then?" she persisted, her backside now against the edge of the table, one hand reaching out into the space between them as if she could somehow halt his advance.

"*Sí*, something else."

He flicked his eyes back up to hers, noting her dilated pupils before closing the distance between them completely. The hand she'd held in front of her brushed against his belly, then rode up the surface of his shirt to his chest, leaving an electric trail of heat. Rey slid one arm around her slender waist, and pulled her against his hips before lowering his head and taking her lips with his own. The instant his lips touched hers he knew it was not Sara Woodville in his arms.

Six

Kissing Sara had always been pleasant—fun, even. But this, this was something else altogether. It was all-consuming and lit a fire inside him that burned brighter and hotter than anything he'd experienced before. And, as it continued, drove all rational thought and conscience from his mind leaving him only open to glorious sensation.

The taste of her generous mouth filled his senses, stoking his hunger to flaming levels of demanding need. And because he could, he took more. His tongue stroked the seam of her lips until they parted, then swept inside her to lay claim without dispute. Logically, he knew he should stop—should demand to know who she was and what she was doing pretending to be Sara—but logic had no place here and now.

Her body melded against his, her hips meshed against his lower body, her mound pressing against his hardness and inciting an ache that threatened to consume him. While he continued to hold her firm against his body, his other hand reached up and tangled in her glorious hair, and he coaxed her head back a little more, allowing him a clear angle to the smooth curve of her throat.

Even her skin tasted like more. A subtle blend of sweetness and flowers that made heat pool heavily in his groin. His lips blazed a trail from the corner of her mouth down across her jawline until he reached the tiny hollow behind her ear. His tongue flicked over her skin and she moaned—an uncontrolled, instinctive sound that reverberated through his ears and sent his heart rate soaring.

He felt her hand on his chest, her fingers clenched in the fabric of his shirt, her other hand now curled behind his neck, holding him to her, anchoring him.

Dios, he wanted more than this. He wanted to taste all of her. To discover if her hidden places were as deliciously sweet as those he'd tasted now.

Tremors shook his body as he left a hot path of kisses down her throat and the hollow at the base of her neck. Again, he flicked his tongue against her skin. As before, the intoxicating elixir of the flavor of her sent hunger clawing through him.

Both her hands were now knotted in the short strands of his hair and the pleasure/pain of it added a new dimension to their embrace. He lifted his head and captured her mouth once more. Starving now for the taste of her, for the softness of her lips, the heat and wetness of her tongue as it met his and tangled in a duel that knew no losers.

This was passion. This was absolute. His body knew it even as his mind struggled to equate the reality of the ardent, hotblooded woman pressed against him—her hunger equal to his own—with the skittish creature who'd kept him at arm's length for weeks.

He couldn't stop kissing her, consuming her. He just couldn't get enough of the taste and texture and feel of her. The hand he'd kept at the small of her back coasted lower, over the curve of her buttocks. She felt different from the Sara he knew. The same general size, yet there was a hardness missing from her body. The tensile strength of an event rider gone, and in its place an enticing edge of softness. Not that there was anything out of condition about her body. To the contrary. She felt lithe and strong, yet yielding in all the right places.

No. This was definitely not Sara Woodville. It couldn't be. But then who was she?

Slowly, he loosened his embrace and tempered the heat in his caresses until he could gently push her away. Her eyelids slowly fluttered open, her gray eyes reminding him of a stormy, turbulent sky right before a storm. Her lips were slightly swollen, still moist and parted. Still inviting him to sup at their softness.

Reynard fought with his instincts, overcoming them with the cold reality that she was not who he'd thought, and driven by the need to find out exactly who she really was. His family had been the target of scammers before—people who thought, for whatever reason, that they deserved a slice of the wealth that made up the del Castillo fortune. He'd developed an instinct for them. One that had saved him and his family much heartache. The fact she had slipped under his radar was disconcerting, but he knew he daren't show his hand too early.

"I have to go, but I'll see you tomorrow, yes?"

"Yes," she said, her voice slightly hoarse, as if words were more than she could handle right now.

Somehow he found the strength to tear his gaze from her face and to drop his hands back to his sides and walk to the front door. As he drove away, he tried to make sense of what had just happened. It was difficult with his heart still racing, his blood still hot in his veins and an erection that demanded to be assuaged.

She looked like Sara, sounded like Sara—even moved the same way—but she was definitely not Sara. He'd wager his life on it.

He racked his memory, trying to think of what he knew of Sara Woodville beyond her talent as an equestrian, beyond her flaming beauty that drew looks and turned heads wherever she went. She'd mentioned family in New Zealand, he was sure of it. A sister, perhaps? Yes, a sister. They'd both competed in equestrian events as teenagers but Sara had stayed with the sport, going so far as to qualify to represent her country—as she had done while here on Isla Sagrado, when he'd met her. But the sister? He shook his head as he tried to force the memory from his brain.

By the time he'd pulled into the underground car park at his apartment building and ridden the lift to the penthouse—overlooking Puerto Seguro's harbor lights— his blood had finally begun to cool, but he was no closer to an answer. Still, how difficult could it be in this wonderful Internet age, he wondered, to find out just how close a sister Sara Woodville had?

It was only a matter of minutes before he had the information he needed. He stared at the search results on his computer screen and sipped slowly at the delicious red del Castillo Tempranillo wine he'd poured for himself while his computer booted up.

An identical twin.

He oughtn't to have been surprised, yet somehow the news still came as a shock to him. So, *Sarina* Woodville was standing in for her twin sister—an engaged Sarina Woodville at that, if the notice showing her and her fiancé in a local paper was any indicator. So why was she here instead; and where the hell was Sara? What scheme lay behind those identically beautiful faces? The web information he'd attained showed they came from fairly humble beginnings. Clearly, money was an enticement—how else would they maintain the kind of lifestyle and extravagance he'd seen Sara indulge in? Her riding sponsorship could only go so far and eventing was an expensive sport.

Even though the del Castillo wealth had diminished somewhat over the years—the result of the curse in action, as *Abuelo* would insist, Reynard thought with an ironic curve of his lips—the family was very well-placed in Sagradan society. And they were definitely wealthy enough to attract a scam. Estella Martinez had been a perfect example of that. Maybe in this case, the twins had decided that two scammers were better than one?

Anger welled from deep within. Slow and determined and gathering momentum until his body vibrated with suppressed energy. How dare they assume they could hoodwink his family? There was one thing he knew they would learn—no del Castillo would ever tolerate being played for a fool. No scandal had previously destroyed them; it had only made them stronger.

He thought for a moment of *Abuelo*, of his current infirmity and the ever present risk of another stroke. Was that going to be their angle? he thought. Were they going to somehow lure him into trouble and then threaten to expose him to his grandfather? Risk an old man's health, his fears of an ancient curse and the ghost of a governess who'd been dead three hundred years, for the sake of money?

What was their aim? Did they think they could use their switch to make him look a fool? Engaged to one woman while possibly bedding another? Was that how they planned to use their switch for financial gain? The papers would lap it up, paying huge money for exclusive rights to the story. Or was their aim like Estella's? To threaten to expose the story in a bid to get more money to keep quiet?

Anyone who knew his family knew that they would do anything to protect their own. And that was exactly what he was going to do. Protect his family—and if that meant ensuring he became a great deal closer to this Sarina Woodville, he'd do whatever it took.

Reynard took another sip of his wine, savoring the flavor, and allowing his mind to roam. Yes, he knew exactly what tack he'd take now that he had the upper hand in this charade the Woodville sisters were employing. They would discover they had met their match, and as his lethal anger came under control, he began to find himself strangely exhilarated by the upcoming challenge.

Rina looked at her reflection through bleary eyes. Last night had been the worst she'd had since arriving on the island. The worst since Jacob had broken off their engagement, actually.

Sara had called late in the night. The line had been bad, reception patchy at best, but her message had been quite clear. Whatever she was going through was taking a massive emotional toll on her and she was relying on Rina to keep things together in Isla Sagrado for her. To keep up the charade until she was strong enough to come back. Wracked with guilt over the kiss she had shared with Rey, a kiss she'd wished could go on forever, Rina had promised she'd do whatever it took.

Her sister had called upon her for help, albeit in typical Sara fashion with all too little notice and even less detail, and Rina had betrayed her. Worse, she'd actively enjoyed it.

Rina pressed her fingers to her lips, the memory of

Rey's mouth against hers still too vivid in her mind. She'd succumbed to his touch as if she'd been made for him and him alone, and in doing so she'd broken every unwritten law of sisterhood. She'd kissed her sister's fiancé and, God help her, she wanted to do it again. In fact, she wanted more than that. She wanted all of him, over and over again.

She reached for the taps over the white porcelain sink and turned on the cold water with a sharp twist of a shaking hand. This was all wrong. She and Sara had never been attracted to the same man before. They hadn't even so much as liked the same type, let alone ever had to worry about poaching on one another's ground.

But she'd done more than poach now and, somehow, without letting the truth come out, Rina had to find a way to step back and prevent anything like last night's kiss ever happening again. If it did, Rina knew she could never forgive herself.

She bent over the basin and splashed liberal amounts of cold water directly over her face, scrubbing at her skin with her bare hands until her cheeks tingled. She reached for a towel and wiped her face dry before looking at herself in the mirror once more. It was no good. She looked just as tired and disgusted with herself as she had when she'd woken.

The sound of the cottage's phone ringing in the sitting room stirred her to action. Please, please, let it be Sara calling to put her out of her misery, she prayed silently.

"Hello?" she answered, lifting the near museum quality handset from its cradle.

"Good morning, *mi corazon*."

Rey's voice flooded through the phone, as rich and liquid as warm dark chocolate. Instantly, she felt every nerve in her body react and hone in on the deliciously deep timbre—as if just the sound of his voice could reach through the telephone wires and stroke the surface of her skin.

Her nipples pebbled into tight aching buds against the surface of the old T-shirt she'd continued to wear to bed each night—the soft fabric a caress as light as a lover's touch against the taut peaks. Heat streaked, like lightning, through her body, centering low and deep in her body. Creating a throbbing need that all the cold water in the world could not extinguish.

"I trust you slept well last night," Rey continued, oblivious to her traitorous body's reaction. "I thought that you might like to see a little more of the island today. Perhaps in the late afternoon?"

Rina gathered her scattered thoughts and forced them into words through lips that were suddenly dry and uncooperative.

"Late afternoon?"

"*Sí,*" he replied. "I will see Benedict this morning for a while, and again this afternoon, but I must also now attend to my office for some hours. I thought to pick you up around four or five and we could drive along the coast before coming back to my apartment for dinner. What do you say?"

His apartment? Dinner? Was that all he asked? She knew that he and Sara had not yet been intimate together; a fact that still surprised her given their engagement. But did he plan to change all that tonight? And if he did, would she have the strength, let alone the will, to discourage him?

"Sara?" he prompted, and she could hear the smile in his voice.

"Yes…yes, that sounds lovely," she finally spoke. At least she would have the day to herself. Time enough, hopefully, to shore up her defenses against her forbidden attraction to him. "Um, should I wear anything speical?"

"Good question," he answered. "We might go out for a drink along the harborside, first, so something a bit dressy, perhaps. What about what you wore the night I proposed? You always look beautiful in that. Until this afternoon, then. *Hasta luego*."

Even after he'd hung up, Rina still stood there holding the phone to her ear. Her fingers clenched around the old black plastic, which creaked in protest at her white-knuckled grip. The dress she wore the night he proposed—the dress *Sara* wore, that is. What on earth was she to do? She had no idea which one it was and, without any contact from Sara, no way of finding out, either.

Numbly, she replaced the phone in its cradle and walked back to the bedroom to throw open the wardrobe doors. Given its rather frugal size, and the number of clothes Sara had kept here, it shouldn't be impossible to narrow it down—but what if her twin had taken the dress with her?

Rina slumped onto the edge of the bed and stared unseeingly at the contents of her sister's closet. Her eyes began to burn with unexpected tears. Suddenly this stupid charade was all too much. She loved her sister with an affection that transcended most sibling boundaries—would give her life for Sara's if necessary—but continuing to masquerade as her twin this time around was taking a toll she'd never anticipated.

Maybe she should come clean. Tell Reynard the truth about what had happened. Let him know that Sara was suffering cold feet and that she'd asked Rina to stand in for her—after all, he deserved the truth. As one who'd been lied to and cheated on, she knew with personal understanding how cruel that type of behavior was.

But Sara had her reasons for wanting to perpetuate this falsehood. Reasons she hadn't seen fit to disclose yet to

Rina. And blood was thicker than water. Rina had never had any cause to doubt her sister's choices before—had never been in open conflict with her, ever. Regardless of her original intention to stop this charade in its tracks, Sara needed her to do this for her and do it she must, whatever the price, because, if their situation had been reversed, Rina had no doubt Sara would step in for her.

She got up off the bed and fingered the clothes hanging neatly in the closet, wondering which dress it was that Sara had worn when she'd accepted Rey's proposal—or if it was even in here at all. She shook her head. She was being silly. She didn't have to worry. It would be a simple matter to say the dress was at the cleaners or that she'd spilled makeup on it or something like that.

She could do this. For Sara she could do anything. She just had to remind herself of the mini-adventures they'd conducted when they were younger, standing in for one another. Though, this felt entirely different. This time, for the first time, she wanted what her sister had with a longing she had never experienced with such intensity. Walking away from Reynard after this, and leaving him to Sara, was going to be the toughest thing she'd had to do, ever.

Rina spied her suitcase shoved in the bottom of the wardrobe and knew exactly what she'd wear tonight. The dress she'd bought once she'd made her mind up to come here to lick her metaphorical wounds, supported by her sister's tender love and care, was an aberration to her usual style. If anything, it was far more like something her party-mad sister would have chosen for herself.

Shorter than the type of dress she'd worn since she'd started going out with Jacob, the dark periwinkle blue fabric skimmed her thighs with flirty layers of hand painted chiffon and the softly draping cowl neck dropped from tiny spaghetti straps to give a hint of the swell of her breasts.

She'd even bought a special strapless bra to wear with it, and in a fit of extravagance, matching G-string panties. The second she'd tried on the dress in the store, she'd known it was perfect for her. She'd instantly felt empowered again, feminine and strong. Certainly not like a woman whose fiancé had only thought to let her know he'd be marrying someone else a week out from their proposed wedding date.

Yes, she might be pretending to be someone else, but she'd be doing it in her own clothes and wearing her own silver-strapped high-heeled sandals at the same time. And she'd do it with all the flair she could muster. Even as she made the decision to be herself, she felt conflicted. In the past, pretending to be her sister had been all about exactly that—being Sara. Was she treading too fine a line now?

Seven

By the time four o'clock rolled around, Rina was just about climbing the walls with frustration. The day had stretched out for what felt like forever and, with the cottage being as isolated as it was, there was little she could do to fill her time.

In the end, she'd taken out her frustration on the weeds along the front wall and in the gardens that bordered the front of the house—moving a sun umbrella along with her as she worked. At least she could see she'd been effective at something through the course of the day. The dry soil had made pulling weeds easy, though, and the job hadn't taken as long as she'd expected. Not even a long pampering session in the cottage's bathroom had filled enough hours before she could begin to expect Rey's arrival.

As the hands on the mantel clock had wound their way slowly between four and five o'clock, Rina found herself straining her ears to listen for the sound of Rey's car approaching. She smoothed the skirt of her dress for what was probably the twentieth time and checked the mantel clock again.

Finally, as the clock delicately chimed the quarter hour, she heard the muted roar of Rey's car as it pulled up outside the cottage. She grabbed her silver clutch bag and secured the cottage's front door before meeting him on the path at the front.

"You've been busy today," Rey commented, looking at the evidence of her work in the gardens.

Rina shrugged. "I had to do something or I'd have gone mad. I'm not used to doing nothing."

"I thought that was the purpose of a holiday? Especially one on a Mediterranean island," he said with a quirk of one brow.

Inwardly, she cringed. Sara would never have worked in the garden. It wasn't as if she wasn't prepared to work hard at the things that interested her, especially her horses, but gardens? She'd made a terrible faux pas in finding a relief for her boredom today.

Hoping like mad that she could carry it off, she gave Rey a bright smile and waved a hand in the general direction of the garden. "Well, you know me. Once I get my mind fixed on something I won't let up."

Rey gave a short laugh. "Isn't that the truth," he agreed. "Come here and let me see you properly. I haven't seen you wear that color before. It really suits you. Especially with the color you've caught in your skin today."

He took one of her hands in his and gave her a gentle twirl—not an easy feat in her high heels on the cobbled path.

"There was a stain on my other outfit, so I improvised," Rina said, averting her eyes and hoping a telltale flush wouldn't blotch her chest and neck at the lie.

"I'm glad," he said giving her a longer, more appreciative look that sent a sizzle of awareness straight through her. "I like this better. The color—" he paused a moment "—is more you."

Rina felt a trickle of unease creep along her spine. His ever so slight emphasis on the word "you" made her wonder if she'd taken too much of a risk in choosing to wear something that so completely reflected her real personality. Not something that Jacob would have approved of, not something that Sara, in her flamboyance, would have chosen—something that was unmistakably her. But then Rey tugged her hand and pulled her along the path to the car waiting outside the gate and settled her into the passenger seat.

She was being fanciful, she rationalized. Her own guilt at taking advantage of him, and his relationship with her sister, was making her see things in statements that were simply not there at all.

Rina cast a sideways glance at him as he dropped into his seat and put on his seat belt. He was wearing sharply creased black trousers that tautened across his thighs as he eased the car into gear. Beneath the finely woven fabric she could almost make out the delineation of his quad muscles, their lean strength a fluid movement beneath the material. In normal circumstances, as his real fiancée, she'd have the palm of her hand resting just there—be feeling the flex and release of those muscles as he changed gears on the high performance engine.

Her palm tingled just thinking about it, and she forced herself to turn her head away and stare out the side window at the scenery as they passed by. Sara would kill her. It wasn't part of the plan that she should be so powerfully attracted to him. It made no logical sense at all. He wasn't her type. He was too…too everything.

She tried to pull a picture of Jacob into her mind, to overprint the finely boned features of Rey's face and his fascinating hazel eyes with Jacob's fairer skin, broader forehead and pale blue eyes. It had only been three weeks since they'd shared that last meal together, since they'd ended their plans to marry on such a painfully civilized note.

Rina couldn't imagine Rey being quite so civilized if the situation had been his. There'd be fire in his eyes, rather than relief that she hadn't made a scene. There'd be challenge—demand. He wouldn't have made their five year relationship sound like a board meeting when encapsulating the reasons why he'd found it necessary to have a last minute fling. A fling that had rapidly turned into something more. A fling that had signaled the end of the plans they'd so painstakingly made together.

No, Reynard del Castillo was a different kettle of fish altogether. Rina risked another glance in his direction, and a warm flush of something she didn't want to name pulsed through her as he met her gaze and gave her a half smile before giving his attention back to the road.

For the first time in days she realized that thinking about Jacob didn't hurt anymore and that, despite her initial shock and pain, he'd done the right thing in ending their engagement. Of course, his method and timing still left a great deal to be desired, but could she honestly tell herself that a single glance from him had ever—in all the time they'd been together—had the power to elicit a reaction like the one still thrumming through her from Rey's smile? She'd be lying if she said yes.

Which left her in a very precarious position. Clearly, Sara's engagement to Reynard had been a fresh new thing for them both. Rina knew full well how alluring Sara could be; she'd watched her in action often enough. But Sara and

Rey hadn't even slept together, for goodness' sake. Who got engaged on what had apparently been such a platonic relationship to date? Was Sara playing hard to get? Was that what had coaxed the proposal from Rey all along? And if she was having second thoughts, why on earth had she simply not said so to him, rather than indulge in this subterfuge?

Something just didn't ring true, but until Sara divulged more details, there really was nothing she could do but continue the pretense—no matter the travesty it made of her own feelings.

"You're very quiet today. Everything all right?" Rey's voice broke into her thoughts.

"Just thinking, really. Nothing important."

"We will be at the waterfront soon. We'll leave the car at my apartment building and we can walk there for a predinner drink."

"That sounds lovely. I'm looking forward to it."

"As am I."

He gave her a slow wink and again that throbbing pulse beat through her, accompanied this time by a pull from deep within her body. She gave herself a mental shake. This wasn't for her benefit, it was for Sara's, she told herself sternly. She had no right to feel this way, to react this way, to wish that things could be different and that she could explore these new sensations he elicited in her.

"I don't know how well these shoes will bear up to much walking, though. I hope it's not far."

Rey cast a quick glance at her feet and gave a short laugh. "Don't worry, I'll be there to carry you if necessary."

The thought of his strong arms around her, holding her, carrying her—it was getting to be too much. She forced an answering laugh from a throat that had suddenly grown too tight.

"I don't think it'll have to come to that," she said, slightly breathless.

"Pity," Rey responded, his voice deep and intimate in the close confines of the car.

It was definitely time to get their conversation back onto a safer track, Rina decided and scoured her mind for something they could discuss without it entering into waters she had no desire to swim. Well, no right to swim anyway.

"Do you mind if I ask you something?" she said, keeping her voice light.

"Sure, what is it?"

"This curse your grandfather kept talking about. What's it all about?"

"Ah, yes. Not one of our family's best moments in history," Rey replied enigmatically. "I tell you what. I'll explain over our drinks, after we've done some dancing."

"Dancing?"

"Didn't I mention it? The restaurant is built over the water and the dance floor is one of the most popular in all of Puerto Seguro."

Dancing she could handle, high heels or not. It was something both she and Sara loved and did equally well. Although, she hadn't had the opportunity to indulge while she and Jacob had been together. He'd been uncomfortable on the dance floor and to keep him happy, she'd thought it was a small thing to forgo her own love of dancing. To be able to indulge tonight sent her pulse thrumming in anticipation.

"Sounds like fun," she responded with a smile that stretched from ear to ear. She couldn't wait.

And it was fun. Despite the relatively early hour for entertainment in the Med, the dance floor was crowded. To her delight, Rey was equally as skilled a dancer as her, even more so perhaps, she decided as he deftly twirled her out from his arms and back again in tune to the heady beat of the music playing from the discreetly placed speakers. She'd half expected the restaurant to be empty, being a week night, but the place was humming with activity. The tapas bar was doing a particularly fast trade on wines and beer and the delicious tapas menu which featured a lot of the local seafood as well as what Rey referred to as "foreign imports."

By the time they found a table, overlooking the harbor, Rina was feeling far more relaxed.

"Phew, that was great. Thank you for bringing me here," she said, catching her breath before taking a long, cold sip of the iced water that had just been delivered to their table.

"*De nada*. We were supposed to come here the night before you went to France, remember? You'd been begging me for days."

"Ah, yes, of course." And just like that her happy mood shattered into a million shards. How many other metaphorical land mines would she step straight into before Sara came back? she wondered.

"Did you want to look at the tapas menu, or do you prefer to leave the choice in my hands?" Rey asked.

Rina waved a hand at the sheet he held between his long elegant fingers. "Oh, you go ahead. Surprise me."

Rey beckoned to a waiter who came swiftly to take their order.

"And do you wish to have wine with your meal, also, *señor?*" the waiter asked politely.

"Sara? Do you want wine, or did you want to stay with your water?" Rey asked.

Rina had the impression he was expecting her to refuse

wine. She thought it strange when she knew Sara enjoyed quality sparkling wines over anything else.

"Oh, wine, please. Do they have any of the Catalonian Cavas?"

There, even though her preference was for a full-bodied red, she could be more like Sara if she needed to be. She'd even remembered the district Sara had mentioned, in one of her e-mails, where she'd discovered a new favorite. Rey raised an eyebrow at her and placed the order with the waiter who nodded before leaving them at the table.

"I was beginning to wonder if there was something wrong. You haven't taken wine for a couple of weeks now."

"Me? Oh, no. I'm fit as a horse." Rina tried to keep a smile plastered on her face.

Sara had stopped drinking wine? That wasn't like her at all. Maybe Rey was right. When Rina saw her at the airport, Sara had been a bit off-color. Ah, well, hopefully she would be able to get to the root of everything when she finally caught up with her twin. Rina settled back into her seat and decided a subject change was definitely in order. It was all too easy to slip unwarily into dangerous waters, like the wine.

"You were going to tell me about the curse?" she prompted.

"Ah, yes, the curse." Rey sighed and leaned back in his chair, fixing his gaze at something in the distance across the harbor. "As I said before, it is not one of my family's greatest moments. In fact, most of us would quite happily forget about the whole thing, but for some reason *Abuelo* has become fixated on the topic. It would probably be of benefit to all of us if you understood the background and helped to head him off from his ramblings."

"Is it really that bad?" Rina asked, leaning forward to

prop her elbows on the table and rest her chin on interlaced fingers.

Rey snorted. "As bad as it gets, though I have nothing else to compare it to. So, where to begin?"

"At the beginning, I suppose," she encouraged softly. "Who made the curse, and why?"

"That bit's easy. Three hundred years ago, one of my ancestors hired a governess to teach his three daughters. It's the old story, I suppose. His wife was often sickly, and largely absent from his daily life. The governess was young and beautiful. The Baron was handsome and virile—a typical del Castillo trait," he teased.

Rina felt her lips curve in an answering smile and she rolled her eyes at him. "And was he modest, too? Another del Castillo trait, I suppose?"

"Oh, of course." Rey's smile widened. "Anyway, to cut a long story short, over the years, he fathered three sons with her. At the same time, his long-suffering wife bore him three more daughters. He was determined to acknowledge his male heirs—his infant sons from the governess. So he forced his wife to acknowledge them as her own children, while substituting the girls for the governess's babes.

"As a token of his esteem for his lover, and as the only way he could show his thanks for the gift of his sons, he set her up in the cottage where you now stay and gave her a necklace set with a massive ruby, known as *La Verdad del Corazon.*"

"The Heart's Truth? Have I got that right?"

"*Sí,* it was a family heirloom."

"He must have loved her very much to give her the necklace."

"Well, that is under dispute. Apparently, the necklace—or more particularly the stone itself—was supposed to represent the family's strength and prosperity. It was a gift which was to be endowed upon each new bride. Why he gave it to his lover, well, that is anyone's guess."

"Why is it under dispute? Surely the fact he gave it to her should be enough proof of his love?"

"One would have thought so, however when the boys were in their teens, the baron's wife died and he entered into a new marriage contract with a woman from a high-ranking French family. Some say it was for financial and political gain, but there was no need, then, for him to continue to advance the family fortunes. He was already the wealthiest man on Isla Sagrado, and one of the wealthiest in all of Spain and France."

"He married someone else?" Rina was shocked. "After she'd waited for him all that time?"

"Ah, I see you're a romantic at heart. You think he, a Baron, should have married his daughters' governess?"

"Well, of course he should!"

Reynard shook his head gently. "Such was not the way of things then. A commoner, while good enough to warm the sheets of the noble classes, could never marry above their station."

"That's just disgusting." Rina reached for the glass of cava that had appeared during Rey's storytelling. "He owed it to her."

"Well, it appears she felt much as you do. According to legend, she was apparently crazed with grief at what she saw as his betrayal, so she broke into the wedding festivities at the castillo and publicly accused the Baron of stealing her sons. Of course, he decried her statement but what is said to have made matters worse was her own sons refuting her claim as well—saying she was not their mother. She became uncontrollable and the Baron ordered his soldiers to take her below the castillo, to the cliff caves where cells were kept for unfortunates such as her.

"But before they could drag her away she cursed the Baron and his children, all nine of them, swearing that if in nine generations they could not learn to marry and live their lives by honor, truth and love, the family and all its branches would die out forever."

"She cursed her own children?"

Rey shrugged. "She was mad, what can I say?"

"Driven mad, more like. And then to have her own flesh and blood turn their backs on her?" Rina nodded slowly. "I can see why she'd have done it. But I imagine she regretted it with every bone in her body."

"We will never know if she felt regret. They say she broke free of her captors once they reached the tunnels below the castillo and ran down one in particular that led to an opening in the cliff face above the rocks. The legend says that as the soldiers closed in behind her, she ripped *La Verdad del Corazon* from her neck and cast it into the sea, saying it would only return to the family once the curse was broken. Then she followed the necklace into the savage ocean below."

"Oh, no. That's awful."

"Tragic, yes. Her body was washed up by the waves within days, but the necklace was never seen again."

"And her curse? Has it really happened?"

Rey shrugged. "Who is to say if she has seen her wishes come true or not? The family lines have certainly diminished over the past three hundred years. But that is only normal given the circumstances of wars, ill health and general bad luck. From the direct line of the sons, reputed to be hers—remember, there is no proof—only *Abuelo,* Alex, Benedict and myself remain. And my brothers and I are the ninth generation."

"Honor, truth and love. Those are the words on your family crest aren't they?" Rina took another sip of her wine, enjoying the dance of bubbles across her tongue before she swallowed.

"They are. I didn't know you'd seen that," Rey nodded.

"I saw it on the doors to your office, the day of Benedict's accident. I suppose it makes sense that she'd have chosen those three provisos if she felt her lover had not abided by them. So, have *you?*"

"Have I what?"

"Have you abided by them? Is the curse broken?"

Eight

She had the nerve to sit there and judge him? Rey bit back his instinctive response and schooled his features into a pleasant smile.

"Now what would make you think we del Castillos would live any other way?"

Sara—no, Sarina, he corrected himself—twirled the long stemmed champagne flute on the tabletop in front of her, eyeing him from beneath her long, dark lashes as if considering her reply very carefully. As well she should, he thought. She wasn't who she said she was, so she could hardly harp on about truth now, could she?

"Well, I was just thinking about what the governess said and how she phrased her curse. It's as if she wanted to remind her lover of his family's creed. Clearly, she felt he had not lived by it."

"She had gone mad. Who knows what she was thinking any more? Now, enough of history." Rey leaned forward and fixed her with a stare. "How about you tell me a little about your family? We've had so little opportunity to learn about ourselves beyond the obvious. I think it's time we got to know one another a little better, don't you?"

Her pupils dilated somewhat, before settling back to normal—the only visible sign of any fear. Oh, she was very good at this, he reluctantly acknowledged. If his suspicions hadn't been roused and if the damning information on the Internet hadn't been available, he'd never have suspected any different.

"What do you want to know?"

She was hedging; he knew it as surely as he knew the sun rose and fell each day. He reached across the table and gathered her left hand in his, his thumb gently swinging the diamond solitaire he'd put on her sister's finger, back and forth.

"Siblings? Parents? What sort of things did you get up to growing up?"

To his surprise she smiled. "One sibling—a sister, one surviving parent and mischief, generally. What about you?"

So she was already trying to turn the tide of conversation back to him. He hid his irritation behind a laugh.

"Oh, mischief also, most definitely. My parents died in an avalanche many years ago. *Abuelo* had the joy of seeing my brothers and me through our teenage years. No doubt that has aged him unfairly."

"I doubt that. If anything, I would imagine trying to keep you three in line kept him youthful. And from the way he is with you and your brothers, I'm sure he wouldn't have it any other way. I am very sorry to hear you lost your parents so young, though."

"Thank you. What about you? Tell me about your parents." It would be too obvious if he asked about her sister right away—he wanted to ease her in to it. Get her to open up, let her guard down, perhaps show her true colors.

She smiled and her eyes took on a faraway look. "For as long as I can remember, they were constantly competing with one another. I suppose, to an outsider, it was a rather strange marriage but it seemed to work for them. They fed on one another's need to be the best at everything. I think that's why they encouraged my sister and me into competitive sport. Winning was everything. It didn't matter if it was a game of cards, or the best vegetables, sport or anything. Sometimes they worked together to win against someone else, sometimes apart to compete against one another.

"It wasn't always…easy at home. Anyway, Dad died suddenly a couple of years ago, complications from pneumonia. It came as a heck of a shock to us all but while Mum still grieves for him, she's come to accept his death—and, with him gone, there's no further fierce competition. She seems more settled than she did before. Happier to take life at a slower pace, I guess."

"And your sister? What is she doing?"

Sarina's lips parted and she started to speak but then hesitated. Obviously gathering her thoughts together.

"This and that. She was recently engaged but it didn't work out."

That was interesting—the newspaper article he'd read gave the impression that she was still engaged. Was she lying? No, it seemed more likely that the engagement had truly ended—perhaps because she didn't manage to successfully fleece the poor idiot who'd asked her to marry him, Rey thought.

"She's been working as a kind of Girl Friday for the past couple of years, basically a problem solver for people—she has a knack for sorting things out, raising business profiles where necessary and creating calm where there's chaos— she's a bit of a Jill of all trades, but I think she's ready for a change now."

"You two are close?"

"Very close," she agreed and reached for her nearly empty wine glass.

"More wine?" he asked. Perhaps he could encourage her to be less guarded with her responses if she had a little more to drink.

"Thank you, that would be lovely."

Their waiter chose that moment to return to their table with a selection of the local tapas the restaurant specialized in. Reynard chose several of them and after the waiter set the dishes out, and explained each one in turn, he took their order for another glass of Cava for Sarina and a Tempranillo for Reynard.

He nodded his acceptance to the waiter before leaning forward to select a crisp golden croquette and hold it to Sarina's lips.

"Here, try this. I think you'll like it."

She obediently opened her mouth and he popped the tiny croquette inside, allowing her lips to close over his fingers before he withdrew them. He saw the surprise on her face at his lingering touch on her lips before the flavors of the morsel of food exploded in her mouth. An expression of sheer pleasure crossed her face, an expression not unlike that of a woman deep in the throes of lovemaking. Despite his simmering anger, passion pooled deep in his gut, sending blood to one particular extremity where it pulsed with demanding need. He'd been a fool to be taken in by her pretense for so long. He should have known from the first moment he had touched her that she wasn't Sara. While the twins were uncannily identical, his response to the two of them couldn't be more different. The woman he'd proposed to had never fired his blood the way the woman sitting before him now did with every gesture, every touch.

"That is divine," she said after a few moments. "What was it, again?"

"*Croquetas de gambas,* translated, prawn croquettes."

He was relieved she'd finished the morsel. Watching her eat it, watching the cascade of delight pass across her features, had been a torture all in itself.

"I think I like the Spanish term best. Hmm, *croquetas de gambas.* Yes, I like the way it rolls off the tongue almost as much as it rolls onto it."

Rey helped himself to one of the minicroquettes and let his teeth sink into the crispy coating before the soft filling spilled across his taste buds. Yes, he could understand why she'd gone into such raptures over the snack. It was truly delicious.

"You've got a crumb, just there."

Sarina reached across the table and wiped the bottom edge of his lip with her thumb, her touch leaving a flame of heat against his skin. She sat back suddenly, her eyes a little glazed. Had she felt that same burn along her skin as he had? He hoped so. She deserved as much torment as he could possibly put her through.

"Thanks," he said, with a slow smile calculated to both put her at ease with the intimacy of her touch and her reaction to it.

He steered the conversation into more desultory topics as they enjoyed the rest of the tapas selection. She had one more glass of wine, while he nursed his single glass, mindful of the dinner he had planned back at the apartment, the necessity to keep a clear head. Aside from the importance of keeping his wits about him while he figured out her angle, he also had to be sober enough to drive her home to the cottage again tonight.

Unless, of course, he could persuade her to stay the night at his apartment.

The thought of luring secrets from her while between his Egyptian cotton sheets had merit, he thought, but would she play along? Sara had kept him at arm's length, flirting with him but never letting it go too far. For some reason he'd never felt the urge to press the issue with her, especially as he'd never held the intention of following through on the engagement. With Sarina, however, there was an inexplicable difference. Almost a yearning. From the minute she'd appeared outside his offices, he'd felt a physical connection between the two of them, and it would be all too tempting to explore it further.

The idea took a firmer hold in his mind. How hard could it be to seduce the truth from her? he wondered. She had no idea he was onto whatever cunning plan the sisters had hatched between them.

The sun was low on the water and a new crowd of people had entered the bar. Noisier, more flamboyant and with an edge of careless fun he had no mood to indulge in.

He downed the last of his wine and stood, taking Sarina's hand and encouraging her to her feet.

"Come, it is time we went to my apartment. I have a special evening planned for us both."

"I don't know if I could eat another thing after those delicious bites," she halfheartedly protested as she tucked her clutch bag under her free arm.

He smiled in return and leaned closer to her, his lips almost grazing the shell of her ear as he spoke.

"I think I can tempt you to more, just you wait and see."

Even in the subdued lighting of the bar, he saw the flush

creep across her cheeks and noted the change in pitch in her breathing.

They strolled back toward his apartment building, a mere ten minutes away, and he allowed the silence between them to continue. Far better to allow her to consume her thoughts with what he might have in mind than to cloud them with inane conversation. Outside the restaurant, he drew her against his side, one arm casually draped across her shoulders and his fingertips tracing small patterns over the top of her bare arm.

He felt her skin react instantly, tiny goose bumps peppering the surface, and sensed the shiver that ran through her body.

"Cold?" he asked.

"No, not at all," she replied, her voice slightly thick, as if she'd just woken.

He allowed himself a small smile of satisfaction, but it was short-lived because even as he recognized how his touch affected her, so did it in turn affect him. Desire could be a double-edged sword at times, he mused as he led her through the vast, glass sliding doors leading into the lobby of his building.

He guided her into the mirrored elevator and as they traveled to the top floor he marveled anew at just how identical she and Sara were. If he hadn't been aware of that intrinsic spark of difference in his reaction to them, he would never have been able to pick one from the other. From the lush, dark red spirals of hair, the wide-set gray eyes thickly lashed in black, to the long patrician nose and the full, deliciously sensual mouth—Sara and Sarina were mirror images of one another.

On his floor, he swiped his electronic key to open the double doors, again carved with the family crest, and showed Sarina into his apartment. The carefully carved words seemed to leap out at him as he passed through the doors and pulled them closed behind him. Honor. Truth. Love. It was as if each word echoed in his mind. His internal response was instant and emphatic. Of course he abided by all three. How could he do anything else and still hold his head high?

But what of the lie he'd been perpetuating with Sara? a quiet deep voice asked from within. Could he swear that he'd been truthful about that? Could he claim his actions had been fully honorable? He puffed out a breath of frustration at the train his thoughts were taking. He had no time to examine this now.

"Is everything okay?" Sarina asked.

"More than okay," Rey said, gliding across the carpet and gathering her in his arms.

She slid into his hold as if she'd been doing this for weeks rather than days, he thought. There was no sense of restraint, no physical holding back. Her lower stomach and thighs pressed against him and she curved into his body as if it was the most natural thing in the world to her.

And it was certainly the most natural thing for his body to welcome hers, he thought ruefully as his pulse began to beat that bit faster and his temperature rose. The scent of her hair and the fragrance she wore wound their delicate way around him, casting a spell upon his senses.

Sara had never affected him so deeply, he acknowledged as he stroked his hands over the bare skin of Sarina's back. Sure, he'd been attracted to Sara. He was a hot-blooded, heterosexual male with a well-honed appreciation for a beautiful woman, but there was something about Sarina that hit a different chord with him.

Perhaps it was the fact that he knew she was not who she claimed to be that added that extra touch of spice to being with her. He eschewed the thought even as it occurred to him. It had been different from the moment she'd arrived here, not since he'd figured out that she was an imposter.

He tipped her chin up to his and kissed her lightly on the lips before reluctantly setting her away from him.

"I need to check on something in the kitchen. I'll be right back."

He needed to create some distance before he lost himself in her and forgot what he was trying to find out.

"You cooked?"

She followed him into the large and well-equipped kitchen.

"I am capable of it, you know." He laughed at the note of surprise in her voice and lifted the lid on the slow cooker he had on the bench top. Instantly, the rich aroma of the spiced lamb he'd prepared before heading into his office this morning filled the air.

"That smells divine," Sarina said, coming beside him and leaning over the pot to inhale.

She closed her eyes and breathed theatrically, then smiled.

"I didn't think I could be hungry so soon after the tapas, but I'm prepared to be wrong about that."

"Good, I'm pleased to hear it," he said, giving the mixture a gentle stir before replacing the lid. "I'll put the rice on and we'll be ready to eat in about twenty minutes or so."

"Can I do anything to help? Set the table or something?"

"I thought we could eat outside on the terrace. The harbor is beautiful this time of year and when the sun sets fully, it's lovely to see the lights. You'll find place mats and cutlery in the drawers over there." He gestured to a sideboard against the wall. "Would you like a drink while we wait for the rice?"

"Just water will be fine. If I have any more wine, it might go to my head."

"And that would be a bad thing?"

She just laughed and got the utensils and place mats out of the drawer before crossing to the wide glass picture windows that led outside onto his private balcony. The expanse of tiles with the toughened safety glass wall beyond, allowing an unobstructed view of the inner harbor, had been a major selling point for him when he'd bought the apartment.

He'd loved living at the castillo—it had been his family's home for centuries and he'd enjoyed the sense of longevity surrounding him while growing up, even more so when his parents had unexpectedly and tragically passed away. But once he hit his mid-twenties he'd wanted something intrinsically his own, and he was drawn to the busyness of the city—loved being close to his work where he headed up the publicity machine that was responsible for driving the del Castillo brand, in its many forms, to greater heights.

"Wow, that view certainly is something," Sarina said as she came back into the apartment. "It's a good thing I have a head for heights with that wall of glass there."

"It unnerves some people. Are you sure you're comfortable to sit out there?"

"Oh, definitely, I wouldn't miss the sunset for all the world," she gushed enthusiastically.

The phone on the wall gave a discreet chirp, distracting him from her smiling face.

"Hola!" he answered, then frowned at the voice on the other end. *"Sí,* I understand." There was another pause. "Well, of course we will manage. You make sure she is well cared for. If there is anything I can do, don't hesitate to ask. Anything, do you understand? *Adios."*

Slowly he replaced the receiver and rubbed his hands across his eyes.

"Is it Benedict, is something wrong?" Sarina asked.

"No." He sighed. "It isn't Benedict, thank goodness, but it is serious. My PA has been diagnosed with a ruptured ectopic pregnancy, she's being rushed into surgery now. That was her husband. He's beside himself with worry about her and apparently all she could think of as they wheeled her away was for him to tell me that she won't be in to work tomorrow." He shook his head in amazement.

"She obviously takes her job very seriously."

"*Sí,* she does. She is like my right hand in the office. I could never have spent so much time at the hospital with Benedict if she were not so trustworthy."

"You must be worried about her."

"I am, but I know the doctors at the hospital are among the best in the world. I'm sure they will do whatever they can. I do fear, though, that she will put more strain on herself fretting about leaving the office at what she knows to be such a crucially important time, aside from Benedict's situation."

"How so?"

"Our company is working on a major publicity push for the resort and the winery. Having to get another person up to speed will cause delays." He shrugged and turned to open the fridge and grab the fixings to throw together a green salad. "Still, there's nothing I can do about that. We'll just have to make do, and reassure Carmella as best we can that everything is under control."

"Do you have a temp agency you can call to fill in someone else's position at work and then second one of your existing staff into her role?" Sarina suggested.

"It's a good idea but we're already operating on a skeleton staff through the summer."

"Perhaps I could help?"

He laughed out loud at the suggestion. "You? There are no horses in my office, and the only time my staff jump is when I make them."

"Horses aren't the only thing I can manage," she replied, lifting her nose in the air. "I've been known to run— I mean, I've helped my sister a time or two back home when she's been snowed under. She sometimes needs an extra pair of hands on a keyboard or a fresh perspective on her ideas."

Reynard noted her near mistake in revealing her true vocation. He pretended to consider her suggestion as he ripped apart lettuce leaves and tossed them into a bowl. If she'd orchestrated a reason to come to work in his office, then he might have been suspicious, since it could have been part of whatever plot she was brewing. But she couldn't have anticipated Carmella's situation. And besides, it might not be a bad idea, he decided, to have her exactly where he could find her every minute of the day. Eventually, she'd be bound to slip up somewhere and he'd be in a position to extract the truth from her, and put an end to her and her sister's plans.

"Do you really think you could?"

"I'm going nuts with boredom at the cottage, Rey, give me a chance. If I stuff up, then you can fire me," she said with a self-deprecating shrug.

He nodded slowly. "Okay, then. Starting tomorrow you can be my temporary assistant. I warn you, though, I'm a hard taskmaster."

"Good," she replied. "I enjoy a challenge."

Oh, she'd have her challenge, all right. But it wouldn't be the kind of challenge she'd be expecting. It would be a challenge of her own honesty and truth, and it would be on his terms. Something he was very much looking forward to.

Nine

A challenge? Rina wanted to grab the words back into her mouth the minute she'd said them. What the heck had she been thinking? Work with him? Sara would never have done anything like that at anytime let alone when she was supposed to be on holiday—or, more importantly, enjoying life as the fiancée of one of the island's leading citizens.

She wasn't kidding about being bored, though. Aside from the strain of waiting for news about Benedict at the hospital, at least there she'd felt useful, as if she'd had something of value to offer and add to the family's comfort. At the cottage there was nothing. She'd met the cleaner and been soundly scolded both in Spanish and in English for risking life and limb on the rickety old bike. Now she wasn't allowed to do her own grocery shopping or any cleaning around the house. And she got the feeling the woman wouldn't be too happy that she'd done some gardening, either.

With Sara not returning her texts or calls, she felt as if she was locked in limbo—and sitting still had never been her forte.

"When do I start?" she asked.

"Is tomorrow morning too soon?" Reynard replied.

His expression remained urbane but she saw something in his eyes that made her think he expected her to withdraw, or find some reason to change her mind.

"That should be fine. How shall I get into the office, though?"

"Good question. The ideal solution would be for you to stay here," he suggested.

Again she had that sense that he was watching her. Preparing to gauge her reply.

"That could work, or I could hire a car so I'm a little more independent."

His eyes narrowed a little. "Are you sure? You wouldn't prefer to do without the worry of driving in the central city, on the opposite side of the road to what you are used to?"

"I'm sure I'll get used to it pretty quickly. I've driven in Europe before. It becomes logical when you're driving in the left-hand seat to keep your left shoulder to the center of the road."

He nodded slowly, but she had the impression he was less than pleased. For herself, as tempting as it was to stay in the apartment with him, she knew she would never be able to resist wanting to be more intimate with him. There was an allure between them that she found more and more difficult to fight. For the sake of her love for her sister, she didn't dare give in to it.

"It will not be necessary for you to hire a vehicle. There is bound to be a spare car in one of the garages at the castillo. I'll call Alex and see what's available if you're set on driving yourself."

"I am, and I appreciate it."

"You like your independence?" he asked.

"Within limits," she acceded.

If she really was engaged to him, she'd have agreed to stay at his apartment in a flash, but that wasn't the case. Besides, for whatever reason, Sara had been keeping a distance between herself and Rey, and until she came back, Rina had to work harder to maintain it.

Reynard turned to check the rice on the stove top.

"Ah, dinner is ready. Would you take the salad and the dressing in that glass cruet to the table? I'll bring the plates."

Rina did as she was bid and Rey followed behind her in a few moments with their meals plated up. They ate in a relatively companionable silence, given the way her mind was now racing. After their meal they watched as the sky turned myriad shades of purple before turning into a black velvet blanket peppered with golden stars.

"I see why you chose to live here," Rina commented. "It's as if the sky is mirroring the lights in the city below."

Reynard nodded. "Yes, I never grow tired of the view. I wondered, at first, whether I would even notice the stars sitting here at night, but you can see everything when you look for it."

Rina shot him a sharp look. Was there a hidden message in there, or was she simply being oversensitive? When Rey didn't say any more, she relaxed a little.

"By the way," Rey continued, "I took the opportunity to phone Alex while I made the coffee. He has instructed a staff member to bring a car around for you tomorrow morning. It is one of their pool cars so it won't be missed."

"I really appreciate that. Will you show me tonight where I will need to go, before you take me home?" she asked.

He nodded. "*Sí,* and we can make a quick call into my offices to get you a card for the parking garage under the building, too. Shall we be on our way then?"

"I think that's a good idea. Wouldn't do to keep the help up too late." She smiled.

Rey snorted a soft laugh and shook his head. "Is that what you are to me now? The help? Is it not enough to be my fiancée?"

"I didn't mean any offense," Rina amended.

"No offense taken," Rey said, reaching for her hand and leading her from the table. "But just so you know I'm clear on this, I heartily concur with office romance."

He wrapped his arms around her and lowered his head, his lips warm and soft against hers, the lingering, slightly nut-flavored taste of their coffee on his tongue as he kissed her. Rational thought fled as he deepened the kiss and as she wound her arms around his neck, holding him close to her. Liquid heat flooded her body, curling around her like a burning silken ribbon of need which then tightened and clenched deep within her womb in an age-old response.

Moisture pooled at the apex of her thighs, her skin there sensitive, yearning for more. Yearning for his touch. Her nipples peaked against the softness of her bra, her breasts full and aching for him. When his hands skimmed up her rib cage and cupped her through the fine fabric of her dress, she moaned, a guttural sound that came from deep within. She arched her back, pressing her breasts against his palms, wanting to feel his possession without the barriers of the layers between his touch and her skin.

He shifted and his hardness pressed against her mound, drawing another moan from her as sensation spiraled with increasing demand from her core. She lifted one leg, hooking it around his, tilting her pelvis so she could flex against him again and again, slow, firm. Firmer.

He dropped one hand to clasp her thigh and the raw heat of his fingers curled around her flesh burned like a brand. He broke off the kiss, his breathing heavy, and rested his forehead against hers.

"Stay."

His voice was thick with desire, the single word more a command than a request. But now that the moment had paused, instinct no longer drove Rina forward. With the slow consistency of molasses, awareness flowed back into her mind. What the hell was she thinking? Here she'd been only just telling herself to back off, to find that elusive level of distance she needed to be able to carry this pretense off and now she was all but plastering herself to the man.

She pulled away, placed her foot firmly back on the floor and unhooked her arms from around his neck.

"I…I don't think I should."

Rey's hand lingered on her thigh, slid upward to cup her buttock and pull her against his hips.

"Stay."

His tone this time was more beguiling, pitched deeper, his eyes now burning with the promise of finding a way that would ease the desperate ache that now threatened to consume her.

"I can't. I shouldn't have reacted like that…led you on."

"You didn't lead me on," he said softly. "You reacted honestly, as did I."

If she'd reacted honestly, it was about the only thing she'd done with an element of truth in it since she'd started this whole thing, Rina thought desperately.

"I'm sorry."

"No, don't apologize. We are lucky enough to share a special spark of attraction between us. If we cannot be truthful about that, then what can we be truthful about?"

Each word fell like a blow on her heart. If circumstances were different, she'd be free to explore that special spark he spoke of. Even as she thought it, a chilling wave of reality swamped her. If circumstances were different, it would be Sara here in his arms or, more realistically, in his bed.

She curled her fingers over his and removed his hand from her body, every nerve screaming in protest even as she did so. Then, she carefully stepped away from his warmth and lifted her face to look him straight in the eyes.

"Please, I'd like to go now. Thank you so much for tonight. For everything."

He gave her a small smile tinged with regret and turned away to grab his car keys from the bench top in the kitchen.

"Not quite everything, hmm?"

She smiled back, a reflexive action that completely lacked humor. "No, not quite everything, but that's my fault, not yours."

"There is no fault, *querida*."

Silence stretched out between them as they left the apartment and traveled down in the lift to the basement car park. Once settled in his car, Rey grabbed her left hand, and held it against his thigh—just where she'd wanted to place her hand when they'd been driving together earlier. Instantly the warmth of his skin and the bunch of his muscles beneath the fine woven fabric of his trousers imprinted against her palm. It felt even better than she'd imagined.

"No one said you could not touch me," he said, his voice little more than a growl.

Rina tried to pull her hand away. "I don't think that's a good idea."

His fingers closed over hers, trapping her hand where he wanted it. "Humor me, please. I promise, I will not bite."

Rina nodded her assent and he lifted his hand from hers and slid the car smoothly into gear.

His offices were on the opposite side of the city from his apartment building. By the time they pulled into the car park, Rina was fighting back yawn after yawn as the strain of keeping her emotions and desires under control took its toll.

"Do you wish to come upstairs with me, or wait in the car while I get you a swipe card for entrance tomorrow?" Rey asked after unclipping his seat belt and turning off the car.

"No, I'm okay, I'll come with you. It'll help me to know where to go in the morning."

They rode the lift to his floor and he unlocked the large wooden double doors. For the second time that night, Rina stared at the del Castillo crest and was reminded of the lie she had perpetuated. And to think she'd had the nerve to challenge him on it over dinner. Where was her normally logical head at?

The answer was simple. Her every thought, her every decision, was clouded by the man standing next to her. Despite everything, all she wanted was to be with him and that fell in total opposition to the love and devotion she owed her twin. A sudden shaft of envy speared her heart. Coveting anything of Sara's felt wrong—so very wrong. But in this she was struggling to keep her balance.

It didn't take long for Rey to find her a key card for the parking garage downstairs and to allocate her a parking space.

"This card will also give you access to the floors of the building from the elevator," Rey instructed.

"Thank you," Rina said, trying to ignore the tiny zap of electricity that shot through her as their fingers brushed briefly.

"I'll show you where we'll be working. Come with me."

Rina followed him past the luxurious reception area and down a thickly carpeted hallway. On each side she could see into a variety of offices. Some individual, some clearly shared in a more open plan environment. Near the end, the hallway widened considerably into a second waiting area. A desk and computer guarded the entry into another office space and as Reynard pushed open the doors, Rina felt as though she was being drawn into the inner sanctum of some medieval master.

Rey flicked a bank of switches on the wall and subtle lighting brought the room to life. As opposed to the modern and somewhat minimalistic furnishings he employed in his apartment, this was all old-world splendor. With her PR background, Rina could acknowledge the clever planning behind the decorating decision. The del Castillo brand resonated with wealth, power and history, all of which were reflected in the richly decorated space.

Highly polished mahogany panels lined the walls and deep leather furniture sprawled over the hand-knotted Persian carpets that covered the floor. A large partner desk dominated one side of the office, with a computer flat screen perched on one side. Judging by the papers scattered over the desk, this was very definitely Rey's work space and he used every centimeter of it.

The contrast between the ordered neatness of his home life and the rich disarray of his working world struck her as strange, at first glance. For most people it was the other way around.

When she thought about it, though, she had to admit to enjoying keeping her semidetached townhouse back in Christchurch in a neat and tidy state so it was an oasis for her when she arrived home from work each day. Seeing Rey's personality so similarly reflected hers, she appreciated more sharply how much she looked forward to coming home to a calm and organized atmosphere.

In this room, she could feel the energy of the workplace even despite its lavish opulence. This was a true representation of the Reynard del Castillo she'd come to know since her arrival here. Focused, determined, but still taking the time to appreciate the indulgences his life afforded.

She wandered over to the large corner window that overlooked the city lights. From here, she could just about see the harbor in the distance, but overall she had the impression of being able to look out over the whole world.

Heat suffused her back as she became aware of Rey standing close behind her. His reflection stared at her in the glass. With the sparkle of the city's lights a halo around him and his features thrown into relief by the office lighting, she was struck anew by the sheer male beauty of him. His eyes burned under heavy dark brows, his chiseled cheekbones high and leaving his cheeks in shadows below them.

She found herself staring at his lips, at the full lower curve, the deeply indented cupid's bow of his upper lip. She doubted even Michelangelo's skill could have captured his near-perfect features. She wished she had the right to touch him, to trace the sharply defined edges, to reach up and kiss him, taste him again.

Rina closed her eyes briefly, unsure whether in doing so she was erasing his image from her memory, or imprinting it there in perpetuity. She started as a warm hand enveloped her shoulders, long fingers gently gripping her bare flesh. It would be the most natural thing in the world to just allow herself to lean back against the expanse of his broad chest. To let his heat infuse her body. To drop her head against his shoulders and to expose her neck to his touch.

Her eyes flew open as Rey lifted her tumbling hair to one side and with that one single movement, exposed the tender skin of her throat and neck. The image she watched now was strangely sensual as the dark-haired man, trapped in the glass, bent to press his lips to the exact point where her shoulder and neck met. She gasped at the contact, trying desperately to quell the throb of longing that pulled inexorably through her body at his touch.

Rey lifted his head, his eyes meeting hers in their reflection again.

"It's quite a view, isn't it?"

His voice was deep, the sound a rumble of air across the shell of her ear. The innuendo in his voice was as sinfully persuasive as the touch of his hands on her shoulders, hands which seemed to have a mind of their own as they skimmed down her arms and over her body, one reaching up to cup her breast through the vibrant blue fabric of her dress, the other skimming down, over her hip and lower.

Heat and moisture pooled in a flood at the apex of her thighs and she squeezed her legs together involuntarily, the sharp clench of muscles making the sensations running through her sharper, clearer, simply *more*.

Rey pressed his lips once more to her neck, his teeth grazing her skin ever so gently, before she felt the warm rasp of his tongue across her skin. She had no resistance left. She dropped her head back, exactly as she had imagined, and allowed him to bear her weight.

She felt him push up the hem of her dress, felt the warmth of his hand as he cupped her mound, his fingers skimming over that part of her that screamed for his touch, screamed for release.

Rina watched their reflection, watched as the man in the glass eased aside the damp fabric of the woman's panties and allowed his fingers to stroke the moist crease exposed there. She could almost fool herself that this wasn't happening to her. That it was someone else reflected there in the glass. That it was anyone but Rey who strummed her body to a crescendo that remained just out of reach.

And in that moment, the exact moment he touched her most intimately and her senses went wild, came the dousing reality that it should not be her. That she had no right to take the pleasure he offered her. She had no right to offer the same in return.

"Stop!" she cried, her voice a fractured facsimile of its usual self.

Rey's hands stilled. "*Querida,* why stop? I can feel you, every part of you. You're so close." His voice dropped to a whisper, his breath a caress against her skin. "Let me give you this, let me take you over the edge. I will not allow any harm to come to you. Trust me."

Every particle in her body shrieked at her to give him the right to continue, to bring her to a climax that she knew would render her senseless, useless to say no to him, to anything he wanted. But her mind knew with damning reality that she would never be able to face herself again, let alone her sister, if she allowed this to carry on.

"No, please. I can't." She shook her head frantically, tears burning at the back of her eyes.

It was pain and torture, yet pleasure of indescribable heights at the same time.

"Please," she begged again, "don't make me."

The words acted as effectively as a drenching shower of freezing rain, and she felt his mental withdrawal as keenly as the physical. His hands, which had continued, slow and gentle on her body, now stilled before he dropped them to his side and stepped away from her.

Rina turned from the glass, unable to look at herself, unable to look at him and the questions that undoubtedly raged in his eyes, even as they remained unspoken on his lips.

"I'm so sorry," she mumbled as she straightened her panties under the privacy of her dress. Her tender flesh still throbbed and ached. "I should never have let things get this far. It's not you, seriously, it's me. I…" she trailed off, suddenly at a loss for words.

How did you explain to the man who had very nearly brought you to orgasm, that you couldn't let him touch you again, ever?

Reynard rested his hands against the back of one of the large leather couches and looked at her. She couldn't hold his gaze, fearful of the recrimination—or, worse, the questions—she might see there.

"Can we go now, please?" she asked, her voice finally a little stronger.

He didn't even speak, only nodded, and gestured to the door to his office. As she accompanied him down the hallway, Rina tried to pull her thoughts together. She could not allow anything like this to happen again. It had come too close to total capitulation on her part. And yet, deep inside, a part of her continued to crave him, crave his touch.

She groaned inwardly. The sooner Sara returned to this

forsaken rock in the Mediterranean and resumed her life here, the better, because right now Rina couldn't wait to resume hers, far away from here.

But, a little voice reminded her, you have nothing left at home anymore. All your hopes, all your dreams for the future—all gone. Sure, she still had her job, but hers was the kind of work she could do anywhere in the world, with her talents very much in demand.

It was past time, she realized, for her to make a new beginning. Step forward in her life, rather than going back to where she'd been before. But whatever she chose to do, her life was not here with this man. That life belonged to Sara, and she'd been mad to even begin to think she could play with the fire ignited within her by being around Rey.

If Sara returned tomorrow it wouldn't be a day too soon.

Ten

Rey drove Sarina home in absolute silence. His body still clamored for her, the taste of her skin remained on his tongue. He'd wanted to see how far he could push her and he'd found out—found out he was just as susceptible to her wiles as she was to his. The knowledge was galling, and yet intoxicatingly exhilarating at the same time. He was man enough to know that, with only an ounce more persuasion, she would have capitulated to him—yet gentleman enough not to force her. The power lay firmly in his hands.

The fact that it had left his body raging with fire and need was a discomfort he would learn to either live with or overcome completely.

He had no doubt she'd been as enraptured as he. What was it, he wondered, that had broken through the veil of sensual pleasure and brought her back to damning reality? He'd wanted to take her all the way—to ensnare her, for want of a better phrase. Beneath the exterior that was identical to her twin's lay a rich and sensuous nature. If he could tap into that, he would ensure she fell completely under his spell.

Keeping her in his life, in his bed, would make things safer for everyone—and, no doubt, prove intensely pleasurable along the way.

Rey snuck a glance at Sarina, sitting next to him in the close confines of the car. Her face was pensive, a tension around her eyes that hadn't been there earlier this evening. Her hands lay clasped together in her lap and even in the dark interior, he could tell they were tightly clenched. Her posture, also, was taut—as if every muscle in her body was poised and ready for flight—and suggested that she hovered on the surface of her car seat rather than sank within it. Would she run from him? he wondered. Would she decide to cease this pretense and cut her losses? While he wouldn't deny that it would be a relief to have this stupid blackmail business no longer hanging over his head, he perversely still wanted to see just how far Sarina was prepared to take this.

He knew she was shaken by the strength of her reaction to him. Truth be told, he was equally shaken. Overriding that, however, was a frustration that went beyond the physical. He couldn't afford for her to run away. Not now, not when *Abuelo* was growing stronger again and would be permitted to return home soon—and especially not while Benedict was still in hospital, his accident all the while feeding *Abuelo*'s obsession with the curse.

It occurred to him that he should never have organized a vehicle for her. It would allow her all too much freedom when he needed to know where she was at any given time. Perhaps, with gentle persuasion, he could convince her to stay with him at his apartment. In her own room, if she continued to insist on such. Yes, she required careful handling, that much was clear. Keeping up the travesty of an engagement was surely taking its toll on her—even this evening, she'd almost slipped and exposed her true occupation.

It would be interesting to work with her, he realized. To watch how she would reveal herself and her experience when exposed to the del Castillo publicity machine. The concept of a new challenge with Sarina sent a thrill of anticipation through his veins. He would keep her close at hand, set her up in his office, in the room where she'd almost capitulated under his touch.

The constant reminder would hopefully be a sensual burr in her side—the images of the two of them in the glass a tangible, visceral thing every time she glanced out the windows. An inner satisfaction spread throughout him. Yes, he still held the ultimate control over this situation, and would continue to do so for as long as she and her reprehensible sister believed they had him hoodwinked.

He reached out and laid a hand on her fisted knot of fingers. She jumped beneath his touch, and despite the faint clawing edge of frustration that still clung deep inside, a small burst of humor settled upon him that she could react so.

"I won't bite, you know," he said softly, injecting as much comfort into his words as he was able. "What happened tonight was my fault. All of it. I overstepped the parameters we set when we agreed to get engaged so early in our relationship. It would be unfair of me to expect more from you than you can give right now."

"Thank you," she replied softly, her face still resolutely turned away to stare out the side window.

But his words had the required effect. He could feel her begin to relax, sense the rigidly bound muscles in her body begin to ease. As they pulled up outside the cottage and he walked her to the door, he permitted himself the barest brush of his lips upon her cheek.

"I'll see you tomorrow, about eight-thirty?"

"Sure, whatever time you need me."

"Eight-thirty will be early enough." He stepped off the stairs and onto the narrow path, giving her the advantage of being taller than him for a change. "Are you sure you'll be able to navigate your way back tomorrow morning? The roads will be chaotic."

She nodded. "I'm sure I'll be fine, but if I get lost I'll call you."

"Make sure you do. I don't want to lose you, *querida*."

He couldn't bring himself to call her Sara, not now he knew the truth about who she was.

"You won't," she replied, her earlier strain audible in her voice once more. "Good night."

He lifted one finger to stroke her cheek before answering, "Sweet dreams."

He waited on the path until he heard the ancient door lock tumble closed, then returned to his car. Once safely buckled in, he opened up the engine and roared back toward the city. As the car ate up each kilometer back to Puerto Seguro, he acknowledged that the thrill of racing down the road was a poor substitute for the physical satisfaction his body still craved, and lowered his speed accordingly. But no matter how he controlled the power under the hood of the car, controlling his feelings for the woman he'd left behind was another matter. *Lust,* he told himself. *It's only lust.* He wouldn't, couldn't, allow it to be anything more.

Rina walked out of the elevator and toward the doors to Rey's offices fighting the urge to turn tail and run all the way home. Last night had been one stupid decision after another and the lack of sleep she'd endured as she'd painstakingly pulled apart each minute of their time together had left her headachy and irritable today. Certainly not the best frame of mind to be beginning a new employment position, however temporary it would prove to be.

As she entered the main office, the receptionist looked up from her desk and fixed her with a beaming smile.

"*Buenos dias,* Miss Woodville. How are you this morning?"

"I—I'm well, thank you. Should I go straight to Mr. del Castillo's office?"

"Yes, go through. Can I get you a coffee?"

"Tea, actually. If it's not too much bother. Just weak and black would be great."

"I'll bring it shortly."

Rina smiled her thanks and carried on down the corridor that led to Rey's office. She hesitated in his waiting area before lifting her hand to his office door and rapping softly before entering.

He was standing by the window. Of all the places he could have been as she entered the room it had to be there. That exact spot. Fire flamed through her body as he turned and smiled in welcome. A slow smile that lifted one corner of his lips before the other, as if they shared something intimate and private between them and only them. And they did, she told herself. Just not what it could have been—and certainly not what her body, even now, demanded.

"From the look of you, I'd say you had about as much sleep as I did," he commented before crossing the room and kissing her cheek.

"I had a lot on my mind last night," she responded.

He gave her a look that said, "I bet you did," as clearly as if he enunciated the words aloud.

"Have you heard how your PA is this morning?" Rina asked, mindful of why she was here in the first place.

"Resting as comfortably as possible, and struggling with the loss of her baby. It will be some time before she is well enough to return to work."

"I'm so sorry to hear that. Losing a child must be devastating."

"Yes, I told her husband she is not to rush her recovery on our account. He is equally upset, of course."

Rey shrugged out of the jacket of the silver gray suit he wore and flung it across the back of the couch nearest him. The pale color of the suit agreed with his coloring, Rina decided, throwing the golden color of his skin into relief against the crisp white shirt he wore teamed with an even paler silver self-patterned tie. She dragged her gaze from him, from the faint hint of the expanse of his chest beneath the fine cotton of his shirt, and sank down into the other couch. Her legs felt weak and unsteady. She had to get this attraction under control.

"So, your first day at work with us," Rey continued. "I thought that rather than pin you down here in the office, we should head out to the vineyard this morning and let you get a feel for the whole setup, then we can lunch and tour the resort in the afternoon."

Tours, great, that meant other people. Someone to act as a buffer against the shimmer of sensual tension that continued to hang between them. She could barely contain her relief.

"I'd love that. Thank you."

A knock at the door heralded the arrival of Rey's receptionist, armed with a tray bearing Rina's tea and a steaming mug of coffee for Rey.

"Thank you, Vivienne," Rey said as she placed the tray on the low table between the leather couches by the window.

"No problem, Mr. del Castillo, and I've rescheduled your appointments for today and let the vineyard manager know you'll be there by ten-thirty. I've also booked your lunch at the resort for two o'clock. I hope that's not too late?"

"No, that will be fine. By the time we've toured the vineyard and discussed matters there, that'll work out. Thank you."

"Is there anything else you need?"

"No, thank you, Vivienne."

Vivienne closed the door behind her, leaving them cocooned in Rey's office. Rina busied herself, reaching for her tea and taking a sip. The cup clattered as she set it back on the saucer, betraying her nerves.

Rey gave her a sharp look. "Still scared of me?" he asked, raising one dark brow.

"More scared of how I feel around you, to tell you the truth."

"Well," he said, an expression of surprise flashing across his features. "Thank you for your honesty, I think."

He reached for his coffee mug and took a long swallow of the fragrant brew. Rina was mesmerized, watching the grace of the muscles working in his throat, the faint trace of moisture left on his lips, even the ripple of strength as he leaned forward and put down the mug.

"I meant what I said last night. I overstepped our boundaries and I shouldn't have."

Rina decided since she'd already been honest about how she felt, she may as well continue. "You didn't do anything to me that I didn't want at the time. But just so we're clear, I'm not ready to explore this any further right now. I know we're—" she hesitated a second "—engaged and for most couples it would be normal for our relationship to be…" She waved her hand, not willing to verbalize the images that filled her mind when she let her guard down. "Anyway, I think we should just keep taking it one day at a time. Yes?"

Rey held her gaze as he slowly inclined his head. "I do not wish to do anything to jeopardize our engagement. One day at a time sounds sensible."

"Good." She smiled, relief breaking through her. "So tell me a bit about the vineyard. How old is it, what level of production, do you export, hold tastings?"

He laughed and raised a hand. "One question at a time, please. I thought you said you were good for ideas and typing, but you're sounding like a professional."

Ice trickled down Rina's spine. She'd overplayed her hand. Just like that, she'd gone and done again the very thing she was trying so hard to avoid. She had to be more careful.

"Maybe a bit more of my sister rubbed off on me than I thought," she replied ruefully, hoping he'd accept her response.

"Okay, it's probably better if I give you the rundown on the way. Finish your tea and we can be off."

By the time Rina drove herself home to the cottage that night she was both physically exhausted and mentally exhilarated. It had been difficult holding back the knowledge and thought processes that were second nature to her, but she'd done it. Now her mind was bursting at the seams with ideas and concepts to help lift the del Castillo resort profile and to promote the vineyard, and the very fine wines they had begun to produce overseas.

Once inside the cottage bedroom, she switched the tones back on for her phone, and dropped it into her bag before quickly changing out of the clothes she'd worn to the office and into a pair of shorts and a tank top. While traveling in the air-conditioned splendor of Rey's car, or during the time at the resort, the temperatures had been bearable but entering the sunbathed cottage after it had been closed up all day was like stepping into a sauna.

She pushed open as many windows as she could, to let the air flow through, and made her way out the back of the cottage where a deep shaded porch looked toward the cliffs. From here, she could hear the sea. Its sound was soothing after the busy day she'd had. On her way through the cottage she'd stopped to pour herself a glass of the Tempranillo wine the vineyard manager had pressed upon her. It was the wine that had stood out the most for her during the tasting session she'd enjoyed and she was anxious to start making notes on the ideas that swam about in her head for raising the vineyard's profile.

A light sea breeze teased the pages of her notebook as she scrawled her thoughts onto the paper. Eventually, her mind ran dry and she put down her pen, reached for her wine and sat back in the wicker armchair to enjoy the moment. Bit by bit, she could feel herself relax.

The vista from this back porch was amazing. Not too far away, she could see the beautiful castillo where Rey and his brothers had been raised. She'd yet to see inside it but if the exterior was any example, she was sure the interior was a masterpiece of old meets new. Had the governess walked the distance between the small castle and her humble cottage that fateful day that she cast the curse? Rina wondered. Had it been a glorious sunshiny day like this one, filled with light and hope and promise? Or had it been dreary and dismal, the castillo the only golden beacon on what must be a forlorn landscape in the depths of winter?

Thinking about the governess and the legend spurred off another string of ideas and Rina put down her glass and lifted her pen, losing herself in the moment. A sound in the distance stirred her from her activities. With a sense of shock she realized it was her BlackBerry—the ringtone the one she'd allocated to Sara. She'd gotten so absorbed in her day and her ideas that she completely lost track of the whole reason why she was here.

She dashed from the chair and ran inside to the bedroom, shaking her handbag upside down until the phone fell onto the bed. Quickly, she hit the talk button.

"Hello? Sara? Please tell me it's you."

Laughter, so like her own, filled her ear.

"Hey, Reeny-bean. How's it going? Are you keeping everything under control?"

It was so good to hear her voice, but Rina couldn't stop to think about that. Instead her mind flooded with questions that demanded to be answered.

"When are you coming back?"

Silence greeted her.

"Sara?" she prompted, and was rewarded with the sound of her sister's sigh.

"It's difficult, Rina. Things aren't going quite like I thought they would. I can't come back yet. Everything's still up in the air."

"*What's* up in the air?" Rina's disappointment at her sister's words, and the sense of helplessness that engendered, pierced her voice. "You have to tell me something. I'm going crazy here. What you've asked me to do—it isn't fair to me and it certainly isn't fair to Rey."

"Oh, Rey, he'll be fine. He's a player, he knows the score."

"That's not the point, Sara. I'm living a lie, for you. I don't know how much longer I can do this."

"Please don't say anything yet. Promise me, Rina? I will owe you forever for this, and I'll tell you everything as soon as I can. You know me. I don't want to say something too soon to jinx this and have it all blow up in my face."

Blow up in Sara's face? Rina thought, with an exasperated sigh. What about the very real possibility of it blowing up in Rina's?

"And when do you plan on telling me? I mean it, Sara, I can't keep this up. I'm terrified I'm going to let something slip, especially now I'm working with him."

"You're what?" Sara's disbelief echoed down the phone line.

"You heard me." She explained about Rey's PA and the pressure he was under with his brother still recuperating in hospital, as well. "I offered to help. I had to. You know me."

Sara whistled, long and low. "Wow, so how am I doing in an office environment?" she asked.

"That's not funny, and you know it. When are you coming back?"

"I...I don't know. Maybe a week?" Sara hedged.

"Are you okay? You're not in any trouble or anything, are you? Maybe I should come to you."

"No! You can't do that. There's nothing you can do for me here. I need you right where you are. I'll make it up to you, Reeny-bean. Truly, I will," her twin implored.

Rina gripped her phone tightly in her hand and counted slowly to ten. "That's it, then. A week. After that, I'm telling him the truth."

"I'll tell him the truth myself—I promise, I will—as soon as I get back."

"A week, Sara. That's my absolute limit."

"I know. I gotta go. Love you, Rina, and thank you. You're saving my life."

"That's what I'm worried about. Is it really that serious?"

"I'm just kidding. Everything's fine. Like I said, I'll tell you all when I come back. Now I gotta go."

Sara blew kisses down the phone then disconnected the call, leaving Rina standing in the bedroom, phone still to her ear, and filled with a frustration that brought tears stinging into her eyes. She'd really thought talking to Sara would make her feel better about the decision she'd made to continue with the farcical sister swap. Instead, she felt even more confused.

Did Sara even love Rey?

How had she referred to him? A player who knew the score? What score? And who referred to the man they had promised to marry as a player, anyway?

Rina threw her phone down onto the bed and went outside to retrieve her glass of wine and her notes. At least now, she had a finite time to look forward to—a date when all this would be over and she could go back to being Sarina Woodville again.

But what of Reynard and her feelings for him? What of Sara and whatever decision she was about to make? Could Rina really stay here and watch her sister pick up where she left off with Rey? The answer resounding in her head was an emphatic no, so where would that leave her?

And how could she tell Sara that she'd fallen in love with her fiancé?

Even as the truth of her words echoed in her mind, Rina tried desperately to refute them. She couldn't be in love. It didn't happen that fast. She'd only been on the island just over two weeks. Granted, she'd spent a great deal of that time with Reynard, but she couldn't love him, could she? She'd spent years with Jacob—slowly building a relationship, setting plans in place for their future. Even as she grasped at those straws, she knew that what she'd shared with her ex was nothing like the inferno that burned between her and Rey.

She tried to call upon the logic that usually dictated her life, but reason had deserted her as effectively as her sister. All she could think about was the way she felt every time she saw him. Every time they touched.

She knew she wanted more. She wanted it all. And she knew she could never sit back as an uncommitted bystander and watch her twin marry the man that set *her* on fire with only a glance.

Rina slugged back a generous mouthful of wine, relished the sensation of it sliding over her tongue and down her throat, before pouring herself some more. She needed oblivion—something, anything, to erase Reynard del Castillo from her mind and from her heart. Even if it was only temporary, she needed the respite from a truth she didn't dare acknowledge.

Eleven

Rey tried to ignore the scent of Sarina's hair and the way it spiraled wildly over her shoulder, touching his shirt as he leaned forward to read what she was explaining. He couldn't believe they'd been working together for an entire week now. An entire week without touching her beyond a light kiss on the cheek, morning and evening, as she arrived and left the office.

It had proven more difficult than he'd anticipated, keeping his hands off her delectable body, especially now that he knew how responsive she could be. He'd spent the past several days in an uncomfortable state of semi-arousal which had left him irritable and short with all his staff. It was soon obvious they blamed Sarina for the change in his usually easygoing mood, and he'd noticed a certain coolness among some of the staff in the way she was treated by them.

Under normal circumstances he'd have put a stop to

it, without question, but these were anything but normal circumstances.

She continued to carry off the pretense of being her sister quite well, he thought, even going so far as to say she'd discussed some aspects of the new campaign with her by phone before presenting them to him earlier in the week. He couldn't mistake her acumen for Sara's, however. Not that Sara was unintelligent—she was completely the opposite—but there was an attention to finer detail that was imminently apparent in Sarina's observations and suggestions that her sister lacked.

He forced himself to tune back into what she was saying.

"So you see, if we introduce the tapas bar to the pool area of the resort, that will keep guests on the grounds, rather than seeing them travel out farther to find light meals, but it won't affect the bistro and à la carte restaurants in any way. It'll also appeal to your younger crowd and I think you need to look at pitching inclusive packages to the twenty-five to thirty-five age group. They have disposable income, they're more likely to be involved in holidays for comfort and leisure's sake than extended overseas trip like the, say, eighteen to twenty-fives. Plus, it'll bring a younger dynamic to the resort and perhaps even encourage them to come back in future years on family packages."

"It sounds good in principle. Let's see what the rest of the family says when we go to the castillo for dinner tonight. You can present your ideas for the vineyard and winery, too."

"The rest of the family—that includes Benedict?" She looked up from the report she'd been referring to.

"Yes, Alex picked him up from the hospital today and brought him back to the castillo to give him some peace.

The security at his house is insufficient to give him the privacy he needs right now."

When news of Ben's release leaked to the press, both local and European paparazzi had descended on the vineyard and, more particularly, the outskirts of Benedict's home in the mountains, eager for a photo of the debilitating scars that were said to mar his once perfect body.

If only they knew, Rey thought, that the scars they sought to expose to the world were nothing compared to the news Benedict had only shared with his brothers the night before his release from hospital. Ben had insisted *Abuelo* not be told—partly because he hadn't wanted to cause their grandfather any more worry, but more particularly because he didn't want the old man to have another reason to bring the curse back into family discussions.

It was enough that the media had, hard on the heels of Alex and Loren's nuptials, exposed the curse for all the world to read about and had drawn their own conclusions about Benedict's accident. If they discovered Benedict's injuries had left him infertile, who knew where the media would take things? More importantly, who knew how *Abuelo* would take the news?

"But he's just out of hospital. Is he up to a family dinner?"

Benedict's release from the hospital had been a relief for all the family. That was not to say, though, that everything was back to normal. He was much quieter than he'd been before. *Abuelo* had waxed long and lyrical about how a man who'd just faced death needed time to make peace with himself and his choices, but Alex and Reynard knew exactly why he was quiet. It was one thing to choose not to have children, but quite another to have that choice irrevocably removed from you. Compounding the issue was Benedict's adamant refusal to consider the idea of marriage—ever. Who would want him? was his argument. A man who couldn't give his wife the children her arms ached to hold was no longer a man at all in his eyes. Nothing Alex or Reynard had said to him had been able to convince him otherwise.

Faced with the same situation Rey couldn't say he'd have felt any different, although his heart ached for his younger brother. And it killed him to see the light extinguished from Ben's eyes, leaving in its place the reflection of a hollow anger.

"It'll do him good to be among us properly again and discussing business. If he tires, he can easily go to his rooms. Besides, for the first time since the accident, he will be able to focus on something other than his injuries and getting strong again."

"Yes, I can see that. Well, I hope he likes what we've put together."

Rina checked herself for the umpteenth time in the mirror before Rey arrived to pick her up for their dinner at the castillo tonight. She didn't know why she was so nervous. Everyone had been as warm and welcoming as you could expect from a family presented with a fiancée no one had met before. More so, if Aston del Castillo's pleasure in his grandson's engagement was any indicator.

Besides, based on Sara's call last week, she only had to keep this up for another day, two tops. The sense of relief she felt was almost overwhelming. Keeping up appearances at the office and controlling the magnetic attraction she had for Rey had taken its toll.

She eyed herself critically in the mirror again. No amount of makeup could hide the ravages of the sleepless nights she'd endured. Even when she had slept, her dreams had been peppered with replays of the night in Rey's office as well as other more adventurous forays where they melded into one another again and again.

She'd woken several times, on the point of orgasm. It wouldn't have taken much, she knew, to give herself the relief her body longed for, but she'd held back, refusing herself even that release because in her heart of hearts she knew it was still all wrong. Reynard was Sara's, not hers. She was merely a fill in. Using him, even in fantasy, to fulfill her physical yearnings was too close to infidelity, even for her.

Rina had already made up her mind to leave Isla Sagrado the second Sara returned. She'd go visit extended family in the United Kingdom for a while, then return home and begin rebuilding a life for herself back in Christchurch. She couldn't bear to remain here and see her twin with Rey. She could only hope that time and distance would make it easier for her to pretend she hadn't done the unforgiveable thing and fallen in love with him. Maybe then this aching need would begin to fade and eventually burn out.

It was probably just a rebound thing anyway. Forced into close proximity with a handsome man she was bound to accept his attentions hard on the heels of being dumped by her own fiancé.

Outside the cottage she heard the roar of Rey's car, followed by silence as he cut the engine. Instantly, her heart leaped uncontrollably in her chest. In the mirror she saw her eyes dilate, a wild flush of warmth spread suddenly across her cheeks. Who was she kidding? This was no rebound reaction. Her feelings for Rey were real. Painfully, intolerably real.

Rina closed her eyes for a second, hiding from the truth reflected in her image. She could do this, she reminded herself for what felt like the thousandth time since she'd embarked on this whole disaster. She'd made it this far. Another day or two was not going to destroy her.

She went to the door and opened it.

"Good evening," Rey responded as she pulled the door wide.

Her heart caught in her throat as she allowed herself to drink in his presence. He was dressed in an impeccably tailored black suit with a pale cream-colored silk shirt beneath it. His hair was still damp and slicked back from his face, exposing the broad, intelligent forehead and high cheekbones that lent a severe magnificence to his features.

She was female enough to be hugely relieved she'd dressed up for tonight. She knew the del Castillos tended to observe the old traditions like dressing for dinner, which was served late—Spanish fashion. Luckily, Sara'd had just the thing in her wardrobe—an off-the-shoulder deep plum-colored satin cocktail dress. Artful pleating both above and below the sash at the waist gave a feminine fullness to the fabric without creating too revealing a silhouette. It was tasteful while still being sexy, and was just the sort of thing she knew her sister would have chosen for a night like this.

Rina had done her hair in an auburn river of curls down her back, and she'd pulled the side sections up—securing them with a cluster of small diamante clips on top of her head—which exposed the chandelier-style diamante earrings she'd chosen from Sara's stash of jewelry. Rey's look of approval as his eyes coasted from top to toe and back again spoke more vehemently than words.

As the dress was fully boned, but cut quite low in back, she'd gone without a bra and beneath the soft silky fabric of the bodice she felt her nipples tighten and peak in response to the flare of desire in his gaze. She fought back a soft

moan as he leaned forward and a hint of his cologne filled
her nostrils. His lips were cool, impersonal upon her cheek
but the look in his eyes was anything but.

"I think we'd better head straight to the castillo, don't
you?"

"Are we running late?" she asked, her voice a little
breathless.

"No, but we will be if we stay here a moment longer."

Color and warmth flood her face. She hadn't been wrong
about that look in his eyes. His comment was the closest
he'd come to breaching his word, after that last time she'd
allowed things to get out of control.

Rina forced her lips into a smile. "We'd better get along
then, hadn't we?"

The journey in Rey's car was short and as they approached the ancient fortress, Rina was struck by the idea
that a single family could have called the bastion home
for so many generations. It spoke to a permanence and
durability she had little concept of. As a family, they must
have toiled long and hard to continue their hold on the
building and the land surrounding it over the past many
centuries. It spoke to a tenacity and sense of unity quite
rare in a modern world.

"This is quite some home," she commented as they
drove in through the gate set in the outer walls.

"Impressive, isn't it?"

"I don't think impressive is quite the word," she
answered, awestruck by the floodlit battlements.

She heard Rey's low chuckle beside her. "It has that
effect on people."

"You must be incredibly proud of your lineage."

He gave a sharp nod. "Sí, we all are. We would do
anything to protect what is ours. Anything."

Rina felt a frisson of caution run down her spine. Was it

her imagination or was there an implied warning in Rey's words? Instantly thereafter he flashed her an engaging smile, sending her worries to the back of her mind.

"Come. If you think the exterior is daunting, just wait until you see inside."

Rey came around to the passenger side of the car and opened her door before taking her hand and helping her from the low-slung vehicle. She was grateful for his steadiness. The black patent leather heels she'd chosen from Sara's shoes were higher than she usually wore, bringing her almost eye level with Rey's hazel gaze. He placed his hand gently at the small of her back. From the heat he radiated she could almost imagine the imprint of his fanned fingers upon her skin.

He guided her up the stairs that led to the impressive front door to the castillo. They were opened as they approached.

"*Buenas noches, señorita,* and Señor Reynard," the liveried man at the door welcomed them. "Please, come in. The others are waiting in the salon."

Rina's eyes grew huge as she passed through the arched stone portal and into the flagstoned entrance hall. Rey was right. It was incredibly daunting. A massive wide staircase curved up one wall, the wall itself lined with gilt framed portraits. Even from this distance she could discern a strong family resemblance. Rey followed her gaze and murmured in her ear.

"I'm lucky, I take more after our mother's side of the family."

Rina laughed. "Lucky? I doubt your brothers would see it that way."

They continued down a corridor toward another arched doorway. Inside she could hear the low murmur of conversation. As they entered the room, Loren rose from her seat and took Rina's hands, reaching up to kiss her cheeks.

"I'm so glad you could come tonight. Now, we are a real family. Come and sit by me and you can tell me what you've been up to since we saw you last. I hear Rey has you enslaved in his office, of all things."

A pang of guilt lanced through her at Loren's words. *A real family?* It should be Sara here tonight, not her. Rina forced a smile to her lips and murmured something vague, allowing Loren to draw her over to the others.

Somehow she managed to make conversation, glossing over the time she'd spent helping Rey and letting him steer the conversation toward the changes they'd been discussing. This ignited a lively debate between Alex and Rey as he brought up the proposed changes at the resort. Eventually, Alex concurred with most of what had been suggested.

"So, you have hidden talents," Alex said directly to Rina. "Maybe you should stay on in Rey's office. Goodness knows he could do with a fresh take on things."

"If I didn't know you loved me already, *mi hermano,* you'd pay for that remark," Rey bantered in return, saving Rina from making comment.

"And what about the vineyard? I can't imagine that you don't have some thoughts on that," Benedict joined the discussion for the first time.

Rina noticed he looked pale, with faint lines of strain around his eyes. Walking with a cane, he'd moved stiffly across the room before, and his sigh of relief as he'd lowered himself into the deep button back leather chair next to hers hadn't escaped her ears.

She looked to Rey, who nodded. "Go on, tell him your ideas. I warn you though, he won't be a pushover like this one," he gestured toward Alex who snorted in mock disgust.

She fought to control the smile on her face. Being here, being around the brothers and Loren, not to mention the old man who'd been avidly listening to his grandsons and interjecting his own opinions from time to time, was a delight. There was a deep love and respect between all of them. She could well imagine how the family code had come about with them as living examples.

Rey crossed the room to pour a glass of one of Benedict's finest wines and brought it over to her.

"Could you bring the bottle over, also?" Rina asked before turning back to Benedict. When he did, she turned the label to face him and pointed at it with the tip of one finger. "I think the starting point for the wine is to have a sense of unity with the del Castillo brand. It's something you need to consider across the business entities. At your offices, at your homes, I'm constantly reminded of your family crest. Honor. Truth. Love. But I don't see that anywhere in your marketing, for the resort or for the wine."

By the time a maid came to call them into dinner, Rina had expounded on her ideas for not only revamping the wine bottle labels, but for an entire new del Castillo look. Her ideas had been met with shrewd observation and many questions but she knew from the tingle in her toes that she had captured them with her ideas. The knowledge was exhilarating but tempered with a pang of regret that she wouldn't be here to see them through once Sara returned.

Rey watched her from across the room and tried to ignore the sense of pride he had in her as she caught the attention of everyone else. Caught it and held it in her palm as she spoke with a passion he recognized all too easily. She might have tried to pretend a lack of knowledge on publicity and development issues in the office, but here, with a private audience, the real Sarina truly glowed.

She was animated as she spoke, and he felt every cell in his body tune into her energy. More than that, she fit in with the dynamic that was the del Castillo family. Strange that a cuckoo in the nest should appear to suit him so much better than the sister he had actually asked to marry him. Would Sara have eased into tonight's conversation as easily? he wondered. He had to answer in the affirmative. She was urbane and well practiced in social mores. She would have fit in as easily—but not as well. He could see that his brothers and *Abuelo* were already completely under Sarina's spell, not just because of her intelligence and insight, but because of the care and consideration she showed them all. Sara lacked the heart of her sister.

A heart he had become increasingly intrigued by.

Before the idea could flower and develop into something more, he reminded himself of the sham the sisters were conducting. No one did such a thing, in his knowledge anyway, without an ulterior motive. Usually a financial ulterior motive. He had to keep his wits about him and his emotions very firmly in check. Eventually he'd get the truth from Sarina, he was sure of it.

Abuelo insisted on escorting her into the dining room, and Rey was forced to acquiesce. But as he watched the long column of her spine as she walked slowly in front of him, he couldn't help but feel the familiar strands of anger pull at him. She was not just taking him for a ride, she was hurting them all. Loren, with her trust and eagerness to form a close friendship with another del Castillo bride. *Abuelo*, with his fear of the governess's curse and his hopes for his grandsons and the family line to extend into perpetuity. Even Benedict and Alex seemed to have opened their hearts to the woman who was supposedly his forever.

Where had their judgment gone? Alex and Benedict had initially been skeptical of his engagement when he'd announced it to them a month ago. Benedict, in particular, had skated all too close to the truth. But now, for some strange reason, they seemed to want to bring Sarina—or Sara, as they thought she was—into the family fold.

Too many people stood to lose too much by her actions. He had to do something to force her hand and he had to do it tonight. There was no other option left to him.

Twelve

Rina was relieved that conversation over the dinner table was wide ranging and relaxed, however it became more and more difficult to acknowledge everyone when they called her by her sister's name. Especially when it was Rey. More than anything she ached for him to call her by her own name, but she knew that was impossible. No matter what Sara's decision was, Rey was strictly off-limits.

As the evening progressed, she noticed how Benedict began to look more and more drawn. It wasn't until *Abuelo* had retired upstairs for the night, aided by Javier, that Alex and Reynard turned their full attention to their younger brother.

"How are you, really?" Reynard got straight to the point.

Benedict flicked a look at Loren and Rina and shook his head infinitesimally. "Tired, sore. It's only to be expected."

"What you need is to get away from here. I hate to say it, but keeping up appearances for *Abuelo* is going to do your head in, Benedict." Alex sat back and twirled his glass of port between long fingers.

Rina watched him, interested that for all the brothers' similarities, they were each very firmly carved individuals. She knew there was little more than twelve months between each of the brothers but Alex clearly took to heart his role as head of the family, appearing older than his years.

"And where am I supposed to go, Alex?"

A trace of bitterness laced Benedict's tone. Rina noticed Rey's brows draw together in concern. Clearly this was not Benedict's usual demeanor.

"He's right," Rey added. "The media are bound to follow him wherever he goes around here. It's not as if he can hide out at the resort or any of our neighboring countries. Besides, he needs to follow his rehabilitation program. He won't be able to do that if he's constantly being hounded."

"What about New Zealand?" Rina blurted before she could think twice.

Four sets of eyes swiveled toward her.

"New Zealand?" Alex asked, raising one brow in a manner all too similar to his brother's. "Don't you think that's going a bit too far?"

"Isn't distance what he needs?" Rina lifted her chin toward Alex before flicking a look to Benedict. She'd expected him to appear annoyed, or at least be ready to shoot her suggestion down in flames, but there was a thoughtful expression on his pale face.

"Sara's right," Loren interjected. "No one would follow him there. He could go by private jet. It would lessen the risk of his travel plans being detected and ensure his travel is more comfortable."

"But what about the personal trainer he's hired?" Rey interjected.

"We do have personal trainers in New Zealand, you know," Rina commented, semi-teasingly. "It might be the other side of the world, but it is quite civilized."

"Why can't he come with me?" Benedict spoke and all heads snapped toward him as if pulled on the same cord.

"You're serious about this?" Alex asked, a note of incredulity in his voice. "But you should be here. Close to home. What if—"

"What if nothing. There's no more the doctors can do for me, I've told you as much. Besides, I can recuperate in New Zealand just as easily as I can here. Better, probably, because I won't need to worry about you all."

"And the vineyard?" Rey asked, sending a confused look in Alex's direction.

Alex merely shrugged his shoulders, deferring to Benedict who immediately started to speak.

"The vineyard has managed without me all this time. What's another month? It's not as if I can actually work there anyway, I'm still too damn weak. Besides, I can work on a computer from New Zealand as effectively as I can here at home. Maybe now that things are financially looking up a bit again, I can complete that research into the new wine varieties I started to explore four years ago."

"You'd be willing to do this, then? Be so far from all of us?" Alex asked quietly.

"If it means having a chance to come to terms with everything, then, yes."

There was an undercurrent between the men that Rina couldn't put her finger on. Judging from Loren's expression, she too was out of the loop. Alex turned to Rina, his dark eyes serious.

"Did you have somewhere in mind that would suit

Benedict's needs at this time? Privacy is of the utmost importance."

"Actually, I do have a place that should work. A friend of mine runs an exclusive boutique hotel and health spa on the shores of Lake Wakatipu, about twenty minutes from Queenstown by private launch. There's a fully equipped gym, aqua therapy facilities, a lap pool—pretty much everything you need. Above all, it's totally secluded. Only a private wharf, or heli access. Of course, being winter there and with Queenstown the tourist mecca it is, it's a pretty busy time of year for Mia, but I could call her if you like—see if she has space available?" Rina offered.

"I know the area. You think you could arrange this now?" Benedict asked, his chocolate brown eyes burning with intent.

Rina looked at the ornate antique ormolu clock on the sideboard. "I can try. New Zealand is twelve hours ahead of us, so it'll be ten-thirty a.m. there. I should be able to get a hold of her."

Loren rose from her chair. "Come with me, Sara, I'll take you to my study. Perhaps you can call your friend from there."

"When would you want to book from, and for how long?" Rina asked as she followed Loren to the door.

"As soon as she can take me, and for at least a month."

Her head spun slightly at the swiftness with which Benedict had made his decision. Clearly he wanted to get away from Isla Sagrado, but why so urgently?

"And, Sara?"

She turned in the doorway. "Yes?"

"I want sole occupancy—well, for me, my trainer and possibly one or two other personal staff. I'll pay handsomely for the privilege."

She nodded. "Okay, I'll see what I can do."

When Rina returned to the dining room she was bubbling with suppressed excitement.

"It's doable," she said as she entered the room. "Provided you agree to her financial terms, and that you pass a credit check, you're all set for next week. I had to do some persuading because she was heavily booked for the time you want, but she's agreed to transfer those to other resorts and spas in the area. She does expect to be well compensated for the loss of trade and for the disruption to her existing guests, of course. I'd told her I'd let you know and call her back."

"And her terms?" Benedict asked.

"The same rate as if she had a hundred percent occupancy of the hotel, plus a premium of twenty percent."

"Make the premium thirty percent. I'll pay half up front, the other half at the end of the occupation."

Rina gasped. "Are you sure?"

"Never more so. Call her back."

"I still can't believe he made up his mind so quickly," Rina said to Rey as they drove back to the cottage.

"He has his reasons," Rey replied enigmatically. "Thank you for supporting him in this. For making it easy for him."

"I'm just glad I could help." She stared out at the dark landscape and worried at her lower lip with her teeth. "His injuries—he will recover from them, won't he?"

Rey sighed. "We hope so. But the accident has taken a far greater emotional toll than we expected. I think his recovery may take a while longer. I'm only sorry he feels the need to be so far from us while he does so."

Rina reached across the interior of the car and put her hand on Rey's thigh, squeezing gently with her fingers.

"He'll be all right. Mia will ensure he's looked after and her staff is exceptionally well trained as far as privacy is concerned."

"They will need to be. My brother's pride has taken enough of a blow with his accident—it would crush him to see pictures of himself, in his less-than-able state, plastered across the tabloids. This way, when he returns to Isla Sagrado, he'll be his old self again."

"He's that proud?"

"He's a del Castillo," Rey replied, as if that should be sufficient explanation.

Rina laughed softly and made to pull her hand away from his thigh, but Rey settled his hand over hers and linked his fingers in her own. Effectively trapping her with his gentle hold. In her heart of hearts, she wished she had the right to be here like this, touching him. Sharing thoughts with one another as genuine couples did.

She'd seen the closeness between Loren and Alexander. Sure, they were still technically in the honeymoon stage of their marriage, but there was a sense of unity between them that she envied. The love they bore for one another had been evident in a myriad of unspoken moments where their gazes had intercepted or their hands had brushed. It was the kind of relationship Rina had always wished for but been too frightened to trust. With Jacob she'd felt secure. No massive highs, no massive lows. Just stability—pure and simple. Now she knew she wanted so much more than that—was ready to take that risk. Except that risk wasn't hers to take. Not with Reynard anyway.

When they reached the cottage he moved swiftly around the vehicle and opened her door, ready to escort her to the front door. His old-fashioned courtesy was something she'd miss when she left Isla Sagrado. It had become all too easy to relinquish the hold she'd so tenaciously made on her life and how she lived it.

Rina pulled the key from her evening bag and Rey surprised her by taking it from her fingers to open the door for her. He ushered her over the threshold and she bent to remove her shoes, letting them drop just inside, before she moved forward to switch on one of the table lamps near the entryway. The golden glow of the bulb flung an orb of light around them, even as it appeared to cast the rest of the cottage into deeper shadow. A draft of air pulled through the house, and a noise rang out from the bedroom.

"Wait here," Rey commanded and flew through the dimly lit sitting room toward where they'd heard the noise.

Rina waited by the door, wondering if she should start to dial the police. Her heart hammered in her chest. The cottage was isolated. If anyone had decided to break in and Rey hadn't been here... She'd been burgled once at her townhouse in Christchurch. Discovering that her home had been violated—every personal effect touched and either broken or stolen—had left a very sour taste in her mouth and a sense of vulnerability that even now she fought to control.

She'd thought Isla Sagrado beyond that kind of thing, especially with the legend attached to the cottage. She'd noticed that few locals wanted to come out this far from the nearest town, especially not after dark. She'd felt safe here, secure. Now, she wasn't so sure anymore.

Another sudden thought occurred to her. What if it was Sara who'd made the noise? What if she'd come back earlier than anticipated? The fist around her heart tightened. How on earth would they explain it?

Relief flooded her as Rey swiftly came back across the room.

"You left a window open in the bedroom. Some creature must have come inside and knocked the bedside lamp off the stand. It's gone now. It was probably just a cat from one of the farms. I closed the shutters and lit the candles on the dressing table for you. The lamp is probably beyond economical repair."

"A cat? It gave me quite a fright. I'm so glad you were here. I'd have been a mess on my own."

Even now, knowing everything was okay, small tremors rocked her body.

Rey pulled her into his arms. "You're shaking. Are you all right?"

She nodded. "I'll be fine. Just give me a few minutes."

"Perhaps you need a distraction, hmm?"

Before Rina could think, his lips were on hers, slowly, gently coaxing hers open. She felt him push the door closed behind her and fumble the key into the lock before turning it with a click but all she could concentrate on was his solid heat and strength, paired with the incredibly gentle touch of his mouth against hers, of his tongue as it stroked across her lips, dipping and tasting as if she were a morsel to be savored.

"There," he said softly against her lips. "You're quite safe now."

Safe? In his arms, with his lips on hers and her heart racing at a pace that no longer had anything to do with fear and everything to do with the man who held her? She ought to push him away, to send him back out into the dark velvet night as far from her as possible. Instead, she slid her arms under his jacket and around his waist and aligned her body against his.

Rey lifted both hands and cupped her jaw gently, tilting her face to his.

"Tell me to leave now, before I become incapable of doing so."

His voice was thick with desire, his accent stronger than usual. Rina parted her lips to say what she needed to say, to send him out the door and potentially out of her life forever, but the words dried on her tongue even as the heat flaring through her body rose and spread. In her head, she knew it was wrong to be doing this, and yet to the soles of her feet it felt so right. For the first time in her life, she stopped listening to the voice of reason and gave over to her heart.

With a groan, Rey kissed her again, drawing her lower lip into his mouth and gently scraping his teeth and tongue across the full soft skin.

"Last chance," he murmured.

Thirteen

And it was her last chance, she realized. Her last chance to give herself over to sensation—to what she wanted right here, right now.

In answer she dragged his head down to hers and kissed him with every ounce of unrequited love she had in her. Rey didn't waste another second on talking. Strong arms hooked behind her shoulders and her knees and he swept her off her feet and carried her to the bedroom. Once there, he reverently set her back on her feet, trapping her with the heat and intensity in his gaze as he yanked away his jacket and kicked off his shoes before reaching for her again.

The shimmer of candlelight reflected from the small mirror perched on top of the tall chest of drawers that passed for a dressing table. Aromatic scents of patchouli and sandalwood blended with the richness of fragrant rose wove their own sensual spell around them.

Rey traced the outline of her lips with one finger, then

trailed the featherlight touch along her jaw and to the hollow at the base of her ear before coasting over her rapidly beating pulse and down her throat. Her heart hammered in her chest, no longer with fear, but with anticipation.

Rey's fingers gently brushed her collarbone before coasting, ever so softly, lower until they grazed the swell of her breasts. Every muscle in her body clenched. The hot tide of desire that clouded her mind sent a jolt of need from her core and forced a soft moan of longing from her lips.

"This gown is very beautiful on you, *querida,* but I'm sure what it conceals is even more so."

He reached around her back for the tab on the zip, and slowly eased it down. The boned fabric of her bodice peeled away from her like a giant petal on a flower, exposing her naked breasts to sight. Her nipples puckered under his gaze, her breasts became full, heavy.

She stood there proudly as he eased her gown over her hips and allowed it to drop in a dark pool of satin at her feet. Rina stepped out of the discarded gown. All she wore now was the sheer scrap of ruby-colored lace panties.

"Ah, I knew I was right," he sighed, his eyes roaming over her form. "You are truly beautiful."

He lifted his hands to slide her earrings from her lobes, tossing the glittering chandeliers to the top of the dressing table with scant care as to where they landed, then slowly and painstakingly removed the tiny clips from her hair. Once each tress was freed, he gently ran his fingers through the weight of her hair, letting it spill across her shoulders in a wave of rippling fire.

Feeling beautiful, feeling incredibly bold in that beauty, Rina reached out and, one by one, slid the buttons loose from his silk shirt. She tugged the tails loose from his trousers before skimming her hands up and over his chest and out to his shoulders, peeling away the finely woven fabric from his body before tugging it down his arms and pulling it away completely.

His chest was smooth and tanned, the cords of muscle finely delineated—his nipples now taut discs punctuating his skin. She lightly brushed her fingertips over them, felt the tight nubs harden even further under her touch. How would he taste? How would his skin feel beneath her lips, her tongue?

She licked her lips, heard his sharply indrawn breath. She looked up and saw the fire in his eyes, felt the answering blaze in her own.

With her eyes still locked with his, she brushed her hands over his shoulders, relishing the strength of bunched muscle beneath her palms even as she coasted her hands down over his biceps and then his forearms before drifting over his fingers. Mere inches separated their bodies but it was as if a live current of electricity sparked between them.

She reached for his belt, fumbling a little at the clasp until the leather finally dropped free from its buckle. Her fingers dealt swiftly with his zip, then eased his trousers from his hips. His erection strained against the black cotton of his boxers and she hooked her fingers under the elastic band at his waist. His skin peppered with goose bumps at her touch, another sharply indrawn breath rasped through his lips.

She carefully eased the fabric from his body, allowing his shaft to spring free from its restriction. Rina backed Rey against the edge of the bed, coaxing him onto its surface, then bent and drew off his trousers and boxers. His socks, too, took only a second to remove.

She rose to her feet again and gently pushed at Rey's shoulders, sending him back on the bed. He was totally naked and hers to revere. Flickering candlelight danced across his skin, showing the shadows and clefts of his body, revealing that which jutted proud and obvious from the nest of dark hair at his groin. Feeling an audacity she'd never indulged in before, she straddled his thighs. The heat of his skin against hers was scorching. The fine hair of his legs lightly abraded the backs of her thighs.

"I want you like I've never wanted anyone before," she said with total honesty.

The words surprised her even as they fled her mouth. She'd never in her life admitted to her personal needs like this. Beneath her Rey smiled, his hands creeping up to clasp her hips and tilting her forward so her mound rubbed against him.

"Then take me, I'm all yours. There's protection in my trouser pocket."

"You expected this?" she asked, momentarily disconcerted.

"Expected it? No. Anticipated? Hoped? Most definitely. I am, after all, a man with needs."

Rina smiled in return. "Then we'd better see what we can do about them, hmm? But first, there are one or two things I'd like to indulge in."

She leaned over him, her hands braced on either side of him, until her breasts skimmed his chest—her nipples rough against the satin smoothness of his skin. She gasped at the sensations it wreaked in her, and repeated the movement before replacing her skin with the tip of her tongue. He groaned beneath her as she swirled her tongue across one distended disc before repeating the action on the other side.

His hand raced over her hips and to her shoulders, finally bunching in her hair and holding her as she continued her tracery of his body. Beneath her mouth, his muscles clenched and flexed, giving her other, even more intriguing surfaces to trace. Inch by inch she tasted him, working her way down the ridges of his abdomen and to the impression of his belly button.

His skin was responsive beneath her tongue, with tiny spasms denoting his most sensitive spots. Spots she committed to memory. When she slid off his thighs and settled between them he lifted his head, dropping his hands from her head to clench the bedcovers beneath him.

"I warn you, *querida,* I am not a patient man," he growled through clenched teeth.

Rina laughed, a slow bubbling sound that rose through her chest and spilled into the air around them. "Then it's time you learned," she teased.

She reached forward with her hand, her fingers lightly tickling the sensitive skin at the top of his thighs, working her way closer until she cupped his sac gently in her palm. With exquisite care she massaged that so vulnerable part of him and reveled in his trust. Then, she leaned forward and flicked the tip of her tongue against his erection. He twitched beneath her touch and another groan ripped from Rey's throat.

His knuckles gleamed white as his fists tightened their hold on the bright colored cotton of the bedcover, his head dropped back as if he could no longer bear to watch and feel at the same time.

Rina pursed her lips and blew cool air where her tongue had been before repeating the action again, tracing her tongue along the veined flesh, relishing the sensation of tender skin over heated rigid steel. She closed her fingers around his base and firmly glided them to his tip, before taking that smooth head into her mouth and swirling her tongue over him.

He tasted of salt and musk and male, and in all her life she had never savored anything so intoxicating.

"No more, you're killing me here," Rey said, his voice rough and breathless.

"You don't like it?" she asked, before drawing him deeper into her mouth.

"Too much, I like it too much. I want our first time to be together. Every step of the way."

Somehow Rey found the strength to withdraw from the heated cavern of her mouth and to sit up. He grabbed Sarina's hands and pulled her upright and stood, length for length, skin to skin. The texture of her was enthralling and he ran his hands over her body before coaxing her back onto the bed. He grabbed a condom from the pocket of his trousers and tossed it onto the rumpled covers before lowering himself over her body.

As her long slender legs parted to allow him to settle between them, he fought with the age-old urge to bury himself in her body—to lay claim to her and coax her body to the heights he knew they'd soon scale together. But strangely this joining between them suddenly meant more to him than he'd realized. He wanted to *make love* to her—to bring her pleasure and delight, to go further than merely indulging in a sexual act. In this moment, it didn't matter whether she was Sara or Sarina. All the conflicting feelings and emotions of the past three and a half weeks coalesced into one crystal clear thought—she was *his* woman, at least for tonight.

Her hair spilled out around her like a halo of tangled copper. Her slender body spread before him, his for the taking. He forced the ravenous demands of his flesh into submission, wanting to take this slowly—to execute every maneuver with intricate care. He smoothed an errant tendril of hair from her forehead and smiled as she turned her face into the palm of his hand and lightly bit the fleshy mound beneath his thumb.

"Who's impatient now?" he murmured, as he lowered his mouth to the pert tip of a breast.

He drew the peachy pink nub into his mouth and rolled his tongue around its peak before nipping lightly with his teeth. She sighed and shuddered beneath him, forcing him to once again take hold of his senses, to focus on giving her some of the teasing delight she'd afforded him.

He ran one hand over her thigh, to the top of her hip and then along the delicate curve that led to the inside of her groin. His fingers ruffled the neatly trimmed thatch of dark auburn hair at the centre of her body. Already he could feel the waves of heat coming from her core. His fingers dipped lower and were instantly wet with the evidence of her desire for him.

He parted her sweet flesh and traced his thumb over her clitoris, feeling her jolt beneath him as if he'd sent a surge of ten thousand volts through her body. He eased a finger into her honeyed depths. She clenched around him—tight, so very tight. It was almost more than he could bear.

He withdrew his hand, laved her nipple with his tongue once more, then pulled away for only as long as it took to sheath himself. Positioning his shaft at her entrance, he linked his fingers in hers, pulling her arms up and settling their hands on either side of her exquisite face.

She flexed her hips up toward him, her thighs open, her knees wide.

"Reynard, please. Don't make me wait any longer," she begged.

Her gray eyes were dark and stormy, reminding him of the seas that raged below the castillo on a harsh winter night. A fine sheen of perspiration beaded her upper lip, her forehead, her chest.

"Please?"

Her voice fractured as he surged inside her, incapable of holding back for another second. Pleasure already began to flood through his extremities as she closed around him, drawing him deep within her, taking him to the ultimate point of intimacy. He withdrew, relishing the tight clutch of her body, and sank within her again and again until he felt her tremble beneath him, heard her cries of pleasure, felt her body tighten and clench about him until she wrought from him a climax that saw exquisite pleasure radiate throughout his body, leaving his frame shaking and shuddering in its aftermath.

Rina lay in the dark, long after the candles had guttered in their holders, long after she'd felt Rey's heartbeat resume a normal rhythm and long after he'd drifted into sleep.

Their lovemaking had been everything she'd ever dreamed of and more. He was a generous lover and after that first cataclysmic joining, they'd made love again. The second time had been slow and gentle, taking their time to understand one another's bodies in intricate detail, yet with a result equally as shattering as the first.

Her heart expanded and all but burst on the depth of her love for him, on how right they'd felt together. But she'd been unspeakably wrong in allowing their lovemaking to take place. It had been her decision—he hadn't pushed or coerced her in any way—and in making that decision she'd betrayed the trust of the one person in the world who'd always been her rock.

How could she face her sister now, having knowingly slept with her fiancé? How could she face Rey, still pretending to be someone else?

It wasn't enough to try and tell herself that Sara wasn't really in love with Rey. Her twin had been asked to marry him, she'd chosen to say yes. It had been her choice to accept a man who offered her the relative safety of a relationship that demanded little beyond peripheral compatibility—plenty of marriages had been based on less—just as it had been Rina's choice to settle for the predictability that had been Jacob.

Inasmuch as it was wrong, they'd made their own decisions. Chosen men who'd offered the security they'd craved as children. That Rina's choice had been proven totally wide of the mark, with Jacob's eventual defection, only made it clearer to her how wrong it was for Sara to go ahead and marry Rey. But that remained her sister's choice.

Rina curled up in a small ball at the edge of the bed, her stomach a tight mass of pain, her chest aching with unshed tears as she tried to come to terms with how Sara would feel when she told her the truth. And she would tell her. There was no way she could hide anything as monumental as what she'd done. She'd made a choice of her own tonight, and again it had been the wrong one.

She could only hope that her sister would forgive her.

Rey shifted on the bed beside her, his arm snaking over her body and pulling her into the curve of his stomach. Her bare buttocks nestled against his lower abdomen and she felt his body stir at her touch. Even in sleep, he wanted her.

Her sister's forgiveness was one thing, but what would Reynard say when she told him that the woman he'd made love to was not who he'd thought? There was no way she could continue the pretense until Sara arrived home. No way she could look him in the eye and not tell him how much she, Rina, loved him.

Eventually sleep claimed her and calmed her mind, but

not before she'd resolved to face Rey with the full truth when he awoke. As much as her sister's forgiveness was vital to her, his meant so very much more.

Fourteen

As cold fingers of light began to poke through the window in the colorless predawn morning, Rina stirred on the bed. Her body was sated but her mind was instantly tumbling with all she had to say today. She slid from the tangled sheets and grabbed a light robe off the back of a chair in the corner of the room. Hers? Sara's? She didn't know anymore. She'd blurred so many lines she'd almost lost touch with who she was truly meant to be.

She went to the bathroom to relieve herself then walked silently to the kitchen, automatically measuring out coffee and water in the percolator and setting the gas burner to heat. She knew it was still ridiculously early but by the same token she couldn't lie next to Reynard another minute with all the guilt that now racked her, body and soul.

Just inside the front door, on the table where the lamp still burned she spied her evening bag. Inside was her mobile phone. She crossed the room to get it. Now that she'd made her decision, she had to get off her chest what she'd done. Was it too ridiculously early to call Sara?

She flicked a glance at the wall clock in the kitchen. 6:00 a.m. Probably too early but she had to shed this burden before it crushed her, and that started with Sara.

As she slid the BlackBerry from its little pouch inside the evening bag, she noticed she had three missed calls already. She'd put the phone on silent mode last night before going out and in the excitement when they'd returned to the cottage, she'd forgotten to change the setting. On checking the log she noted two were last night and one already this morning. All were from Sara.

So, she'd made her decision.

Rina's heart sank. The very fact that her sister had tried so often to reach her meant that she must have made up her mind. Sara had never known restraint. One message would never be enough.

With shaking hands, she started to dial her voice mail, only to nearly drop her phone when it vibrated in her hand. She gathered her startled thoughts together and hit the talk button.

"Sara?"

"Oh, thank goodness I got you this time. Where have you been? Actually, never mind about that. I just wanted to let you know, I'm coming back today—"

Sara's voice faded out on a burst of static.

"Back today? What time?" Rina asked, the weight of guilt in her chest warring with looking forward to seeing her twin again.

"…so excited… I've been so silly but I reached my decision…coming to talk to Rey…getting married…can't wait to see you—"

Rina's heart dropped straight to her feet. She tried to pull words from her mind but nothing would cooperate, and then, on another burst of static, her link to her sister was gone. Rina's legs turned to water and she sank onto the nearest piece of furniture, a wooden straight-backed chair. The cool of the wood seeped through the light material of her robe and into her skin and a shiver ran through her body. The phone fell from her hand to the tiled floor, the back cover bursting off and the battery scattering a short distance away.

Sara was coming back to marry Rey. She'd made her decision without knowing that her sister, her twin, had betrayed her in the worst way possible. Rina began to feel her hold on reality slip away. Not only had she done the worst thing imaginable by sleeping with her sister's fiancé, she would now irrevocably lose them both.

It was time to come clean. First with Rey, then with Sara when she arrived. What she'd done was monstrous, and she could only hold onto the thin reed of hope that her sister could one day find it in her heart to forgive her for what she'd done. Sara had been clear that she hadn't loved Rey, but that didn't make what Rina had done last night any less despicable. Reynard had given her the choice to send him away. She'd chosen not to. Everything—every touch, every sigh, every starburst of pleasure—it was all her fault and it was time she became accountable.

She forced herself to her feet and went to the kitchen, gathering two mugs and pouring coffee for each of them. It was time to face the music.

Rey was sprawled over the bed on his stomach, his dark hair endearingly rumpled, his tanned skin a dark contrast to the white sheet that curved lovingly across his buttocks and obscured his legs from view. The fingers of one hand splayed across her pillow, much as they'd splayed across her body in those moments when they'd slept last night. A painful tug in her chest reminded her that he wasn't hers to view.

She put both coffees on the bedside table and reached out a hand to wake him. The instant her fingers touched his shoulder, they tingled. Even now, knowing he was forbidden to her, knowing she had to deliver to him the painful truth about what she'd done—how she'd deceived him—her body still responded on an instinctual level.

She leaned over the bed and gave him a little shake. "Rey? Wake up, I need to talk to you."

His dark lashes flickered on his cheek before he opened his eyes, lifted his head and rolled onto his side. The instant his gaze met hers, his eyes began to burn with the hunger she recognized, and couldn't help but share. He reached out one hand to touch her face, his fingers stroking her cheek and coming to rest on her lips, still swollen from last night's feverish kisses.

"Buenos dias." He smiled and slid his hand around to cup the back of her head and pull her down for a kiss.

At the tenderness of his touch upon her lips, the burning sting of tears pricked at the back of Rina's eyes. She squeezed her eyelids shut. She couldn't cry in front of him. Not now. Somehow she found the strength to pull away and stand at the edge of the bed.

"Already tired of me?" Rey teased from within the untidy evidence of last night's passion.

"No, it's not that." She grabbed his mug off the nightstand and passed it to him. "Here, have this."

Rey pulled himself upright against the headboard and took the mug from her, his fingers grazing hers.

"I'd rather have you, *querida.*"

He wouldn't want her again after what she had to say. Rina took a sip of her coffee and instantly wished she hadn't. The dark brew caught in her throat and she fought to swallow it past the restriction there.

"Sar—" Rey started. "Is everything all right?"

Rina couldn't meet his eyes. Instead she put her coffee cup down and perched on the very edge of the bed.

"I...I'm not who you think I am," she began.

Rey felt the familiar boil of anger start deep in his belly. So, this was it? She had gotten what she was after? That was the only reason he could think of for why *now* she wanted to tell the truth. It had been foolish of him to give her and her sister the very ammunition they needed by sleeping with her last night. Hell, sleeping? They'd achieved very little of that. The sex had been great.

A prick of conscience jabbed at the back of his mind. Great? It had been better than great. And it had been so much more than just sex. He'd made love with her, worshipped her, taken and received pleasure such as he had never experienced with another before. Resolutely, he squashed those thoughts. The Woodville sisters had an agenda. When he hadn't been sexually attracted to the one, they'd delivered on the other—and he'd let them. Did that make him a bastard for taking advantage of the situation?

Not at all. He'd be damned if he'd let them screw one Euro from his family.

"I know who you are," he replied, his voice deadpan.

Shock flew across Sarina's face. "You know?"

"You are Sarina Woodville. Younger twin and sister to Sara Woodville—my fiancée."

"How did you...? When?" Her eyes flew to the bed. "Why?"

"How? Well, you are indeed a perfect replica of your sister but there are some things you cannot fake and your sister's nature is one of them."

"But you never said—"

"Never called you on it? Why would I? I didn't have time to deal with your silly games. At the time my first priority was my brother, my second, *Abuelo*. And then you started helping me at the office at a time when help was badly needed. I suppose I've received recompense for at least some of what you and your sister have cost me."

"How long have you known?"

"I realized that you weren't Sara when I kissed you. I knew instantly you were not the woman I'd asked to be my fiancée."

"How?" The word came out in a strangled gasp.

How? He was not likely to tell her the truth—how kissing her sister had been a pleasant diversion whereas kissing her had been an experience that had blown his mind off the Richter scale.

He did not want to think of that now. Nor of the delight he'd experienced when they'd danced together at the tapas bar, or of the intellectual satisfaction he'd gained while they'd worked together. He especially did not want to think of how she'd made him feel last night.

"How matters not. What's important is that I caught onto your deception early enough to stop you when you tried to capitalize on it."

"Capitalize on it? I don't understand. Sara just asked me to—"

"Just asked you to lie to me? Deceive me? Set me and my family up for scandal and humiliation?" He smiled, although he had never felt any less humor in his life. "You see, the del Castillo family are well versed in the tricks of others. You two are not the first to think you can deceive us into what appears to be a relationship and then subsequently sell our family to the media, or worse, threaten to do so to extort money from us. We are not so dull witted that we will allow this to happen, no matter how much stress we are under."

"But it's not true," she insisted. Her face had paled, her pupils massively dilated, her hands trembled. "We aren't trying to extort money from you. Far from it. Sara didn't want to upset you—"

He snorted. "Upset me? You two have far from upset me. You disgust me with your avaricious lies. I know she needs sponsorship to continue with her horses, she was at least honest about that while she was here. But clearly that wasn't all she wanted, nor you. Tell me, when your fiancé broke off your engagement, was it because he'd discovered just how duplicitous you are? Or did you discover that he wasn't worth the bother and decided to come here for bigger fish to fry?"

"It wasn't like that," she cried, her slender shoulders slumped forward and what appeared to be grief slanted raw and stark across her face.

Oh, she was a good actress. He'd give her that. Even now, some traitorous instinct wanted to reach out to her, comfort her, pull her into his arms and take away all of her pain. He ruthlessly pushed the urge away. She was manipulating him again. He would not allow himself to fall for it.

"Rey, you have to believe me. I could never do what you're suggesting. I love you!"

The anger that had been simmering low in his gut exploded into a red haze of fury. It wasn't enough for her that she'd seduced his body and his mind—now she thought she could play with his heart, as well? He pushed himself up, dragging the top sheet off the bed and wrapping it around his hips. His forgotten coffee mug crashed to the floor and splintered into a dozen pieces, dark liquid spilling across the tiles.

"Love? You *dare* to tell me you love me?"

"It's true, I do love you. I didn't expect to—I certainly didn't want to. You're engaged to my sister."

"*Was* engaged to your sister."

"But we weren't…we didn't… Please at least hear her out."

"I'll hear her out, all right, before I send you both packing off the island. You are no longer welcome here. I think you'll find your visa rescinded by this afternoon."

Rey dropped the sheet and stepped into his trousers, eschewing the rest of his clothing which he bunched into a bundle and tucked under his arm.

"Rey, please don't go. Please don't leave like this. I know I should have told you everything from the beginning but there was no right time."

She thrust out her left hand in an attempt to stop him as he stalked past. The diamond ring he'd given Sara still glinted on her finger, caught in the rays of the rising sun as they filtered through the window. Already the heat of the day was streaming in, but inside him he'd never in his life felt so cold. He looked pointedly at the ring on her finger.

"That is not yours to wear."

"I know, I'm sorry." She bent her head and pulled the ring off her finger before dropping it into his outstretched hand.

Reynard shoved the ring in his pocket. If he never saw it again it would be too soon.

"I will make the arrangements for you to leave Isla Sagrado at once. One of my staff will call you with the details," he said as he covered the short distance to the bedroom door. He stopped inside the doorway and hesitated a moment, then turned to deliver his parting shot in scathing tones.

"Oh, and thanks for last night. That definitely made it all worthwhile."

Fifteen

It was well into the morning before Rina could bring herself to move from the bed. She'd curled into a fetal position of silent suffering in the face of Rey's bitter anger. Finally, the worst of the anguish passed, leaving her blessedly numb. Like an automaton, she gathered the sheets and bedcover off the bed and staggered through to the washing machine, set in an alcove in the bathroom. She shoved the linens into the machine, added soap and turned it on.

Continuing to go through the motions, she took a shower and washed herself thoroughly—washed away every last touch or caress that Reynard had given her.

A while later, back in the bedroom, when she reached for the first thing at hand, she remembered she was no longer wearing her sister's clothes. She was no longer Sara Woodville, but Sarina. She bent and dragged her suitcase from the bottom of the small cupboard, put it on the bare bed and wrestled the zip open. She grabbed the outfit on top—a pair of white capri pants and a mint green T-shirt. It was little comfort but it felt good to be in her own clothes again.

Since she'd been here, aside from her lingerie, she'd hardly worn her own clothing. She turned back to the wardrobe and fingered the fabric of the blue dress she'd worn on the night they'd almost made love for the first time. She should have told him then, she thought.

She'd felt so beautiful that night. So desired, even if it was all wrong. It occurred to her that he'd known even then that she wasn't Sara. And knowing she wasn't, he'd still wined and dined her, had performed intimacies on her that had tested her resilience beyond her expectations. A resilience that had broken under his kiss last night.

He'd meant to make love to her all along. A bubble of anger started to bloom in the pit of her stomach. What kind of man made love to one sister while still engaged to the other? Was he so calculated and so removed from genuine emotion? And Sara still expected to marry him.

She sank to her knees on the cold tile floor. Oh God, Sara. She was returning today. How on earth was she going to tell her what she'd done?

Reynard paced back and forth in his office, his mind tumbling with anger and confusion. His behavior toward Sarina was justified. More than justified, he told himself for the hundredth time since he'd gotten into his Ferrari and raced back to the city. But try as he might, he couldn't ignore the sharp tearing pain in the region of his heart as he considered the woman he'd made love with last night.

He'd been harsh in the face of her confession. Cruel, also, as he'd left. Neither state came naturally to him but, considering what had happened with Estella and then the discovery of the twins' deception, what else was he to do?

He dropped into his leather executive chair behind his desk, put his head against the high back and closed his eyes. Sarina's image was branded across his mind. The look on her face last night when she'd decided not to send him on his way. The passion when he'd entered her body for the first time. The hurt, the shock as he'd let loose his venom this morning—each word an individual blow calculated to hurt her.

He'd known all along about the lies, and yet, when she'd admitted it to him, it had roused in him a new fury. Why? He'd known, even when he'd asked to stay the night with her, that this choice was bound to be exactly what she needed for her plan. He should have expected her to tell him the truth when morning rolled around. Why had he been surprised? Had he fooled himself into believing that their lovemaking meant something to her? That she had not embarked upon a course of treachery and deceit for mercenary gain, but had, instead, shared her bed with him for no reason other than her own desire?

His head began to throb.

He forced his eyes open and reached for his telephone. Whatever his reasons, whatever hers, he needed to follow through and see her leave Isla Sagrado. There was no room in his life for her kind, nor his own brand of foolishness in wishing their time together to be any different.

Before he could lift the receiver, however, his intercom buzzed.

"Señor del Castillo, Miss Woodville is here to see you."

Words momentarily failed him. She had the unmitigated

gall to come to him at his office, even after he'd told her that he never wanted to see her again?

"*Señor?* Should I tell her you are otherwise engaged?"

His lips quirked at Vivienne's unintentional pun. "No, it's okay. Send her in."

The instant the door opened, he knew it was Sara Woodville who crossed the threshold. The two women might be identical, he acknowledged as he rose and walked around his desk to receive her—but to him, Sara was a pale facsimile of the woman he'd come to love. He misstepped on the carpet. Love? No. It couldn't be. The very thought was ridiculous.

"Rey, I have to tell you something." Sara cut through any preliminary greetings and got straight to the point.

"This should be interesting," he answered under his breath.

"I beg your pardon?"

"I'm aware of the deception you and your sister have pulled. You can consider our engagement officially ended."

"Oh, thank goodness!"

Her answer was anything but what he'd expected. She was relieved? What manner of con artist was relieved to have the game ended before payout had been achieved?

"I didn't want Rina to tell you the truth, but obviously she has. Rey, what we did was wrong. What *I* did was wrong. I should never have accepted your proposal. Not when I loved another man."

Rey's head reeled. "You love another man?"

"I do. I met him during the endurance trials near Maureillas. We fell in love so fast that I didn't want to believe it was real. *Couldn't* believe it was real, to be honest. It was all too much for me. I wasn't looking for anything serious, you know that. But he swept me off my feet. It scared me enough to push him away. I said some terrible things to him and hurt him badly before the tournament here. He was supposed to come and compete for France but he withdrew from the team and remained in Perpignan."

"Why are you telling me this?" Rey asked, still thoroughly confused. Had the sisters been setting up yet another mark?

"Because you deserve the truth, and you deserve far better than me. When I arrived here, and we met, I decided you were the perfect man for me. Uncommitted, fun, not looking for forever. And then you asked me to marry you. I was flattered, who wouldn't be? But I said 'yes' for all the wrong reasons. I didn't want to admit to myself that I'd fallen in love with Paul, but then I began to suspect I might be pregnant."

"You stopped drinking coffee and alcohol."

"Yes, I'm surprised you noticed."

"What I noticed was that your sister had not. It was one of the first things that drew the truth to my attention, although I was distracted at the time with Benedict's accident."

Sara's hands fluttered to her face, "I can't believe I'd forgotten to ask you about that. How is he?"

"Recovering at the castillo for now."

"I'm so glad. I never meant to leave you in the lurch at such a rough time—I had no idea anything had happened to Benedict until Rina told me. But by then, I was already in France. It wasn't long before I started to question my acceptance of your proposal and I knew that before I could do anything, I needed to talk to Paul again. Things with us were still so new—I couldn't tell you I had to run off to

France to talk with an old lover, but how could I explain leaving?

"Then Rina called to tell me about her broken engagement, and the timing was just too good to pass up. She needed to get away, and so did I. I asked her to visit, and arranged my flight from France to get in at the same time as hers. We barely had a chance to say hello before I shoved the letter at her, asking her to take my place."

The envelope with the ring, Reynard realized. The one that had had him worried that Sara planned to break their engagement. The one that had triggered their first kiss—and with it, the realization that Sara was not the woman who had been taking over his senses. It hadn't been addressed to him at all, but to her sister—asking her to play along with the charade.

"I know it wasn't fair—to you or to Rina—but I also knew that she wouldn't tell me no. I flew straight back to France. At first, Paul wouldn't see me, but eventually we got together and we've sorted things out. He still loves me and I know I love him also."

"And if he had not wanted you? Were you going to foist his child upon me?" Rey was rocked by her revelations, but his wits weren't so completely scattered to keep him from asking the obvious question. Sarina might not have been using him with financial motives, but Sara still could have been.

"I'll be honest. When I first went to Perpignan, the thought had crossed my mind, but in the end, I know I would never have done that to you. Reynard, I'm so sorry I used you. Sorry I used Rina, too. I should have been honest with you from the start and explained why I had to go away instead of expecting my sister to pick up the pieces."

"I can't accept your apology, Sara. What the two of you

have done—it has made me feel very manipulated and very angry."

"I understand. Look, I haven't seen Rina yet, and I need to tell her what has happened. Can I ask you not to say anything to her until then?"

Say anything to her? He'd ordered her from the island— from his life. He doubted that not speaking to her would be a problem. In response to Sara's question he nodded.

"Rina is leaving the island later today. I suggest that you go with her."

"I'm only here to clear things up with you, collect Rina and get my things. You won't need to worry about us again."

After Sara had gone, Reynard's head began to pound. How could he have been so incredibly wrong about Rina? Had his earlier experience with Estella so poisoned him that he'd been incapable of viewing any woman without suspicion? She'd admitted she pretended to be her sister. Admitted everything, including her love for him. And he'd called her a liar and crushed her with his anger.

Yes, she had deceived him, but wouldn't he have done the same thing for either of his brothers? Of course he would, if asked. In fact, his perpetuation of his engagement to Sara was no less a counterfeit than what the sisters had done to him. He'd done it to put *Abuelo*'s mind at rest, but the fact he had done it at all made him no different from Sarina and her twin.

He loved her. The truth of it pounded at his temples, insisting he acknowledge it. More, that he accept it as the core of his being. As hard as he'd fought it, she'd inveigled her way into his heart with her gentle ways, her quick intelligence and her unreserved passion. And he had sent her away. A deep-seated ache penetrated his chest.

He reached for the phone on his desk once more.

Somehow he had to right the wrongs he'd done her. Somehow, he had to find a way to make her stay.

"Reeny-bean, are you there?"

Rina straightened from the dryer where she was untangling the clean sheets and bedcover in readiness to remake the bed. She dropped everything and ran to the front door of the cottage. Apprehension over what her sister was going to say to her confession flew in the face of her initial joy at seeing her twin again.

Tears flowed freely down her face as they hugged one another tight. It felt far longer than a month had passed since Rina had last seen her sister at Isla Sagrado's airport. So much had happened.

"I've got so much to tell you!" they both blurted at the same time, then laughed through their tears.

"You first," said Sara. "Is everything okay?"

They walked, hand in hand, into the sitting-room area and sat together on the sofa there. Rina swallowed against the fear in her throat. Sara would understand why she'd done what she'd done. She had to.

"I did the worst thing, Sara. I fell in love with him. I'm so sorry. I didn't mean to. I didn't want to. I fought it all the way, but—"

"You fell in love with Rey?" Sara interrupted, her voice pitched high in disbelief. "How? Why?"

"I don't know. It just happened. But he worked out who I was a couple of weeks ago. He's been playing me along ever since." She drew back from her sister and squared her shoulders before meeting concerned gray eyes the mirror of her own. "I slept with him, Sara. I'm so sorry. I broke every promise we ever made to one another. I just…" She shook her head and began to sob anew. "He doesn't want me—he's basically banished me from Isla Sagrado."

"It's okay." Sara pulled Rina into her arms and hugged her tight, stroking her hair like she had when they were younger and Rina had borne the brunt of their parents' anger for one thing or another. "Really, it's okay. I broke our promises first by making you do what I did. I don't love Rey, I never did. I accepted his proposal for all the wrong reasons and I should never have done it. And I never should have asked you to step in for me, to keep a relationship alive that I wasn't even sure I wanted. It wasn't fair to him, to me or to you. I should have been honest with him from the start. You were so right, Reeny-bean. I wish I'd been truthful with you when you arrived here, even if it would only have saved you from being so hurt."

They sat and rocked together until Rina's sobs quieted.

"He's so angry." Rina said when she could speak again.

"I know, I've never seen him so distant before."

"You've seen him?" Rina pulled away from her sister's arms. "When?"

"Before I came here. I owed him the truth about why I went away. I owe it to you, too. The truth is, I met someone a few months ago, during a tournament in France. We fell in love and he wanted to marry me, but I couldn't. It was just all so fast, so intense, you know? And we were already competing against one another in the tournaments. All I could think about was how fierce Mum and Dad were about beating one another at everything they did, how horrid they made themselves feel when one or the other won. I didn't want that to happen to me. So when I got here and met Rey and he was so different, it was a relief to just let myself think we could make a go of things. When he asked me to get engaged, of course I said yes. I figured that when we married, life would just be more of the same.

There was no spark, no fierce need, no impatience to be better than him.

"But then I found out I was expecting Paul's baby, and I knew I couldn't avoid the truth any longer. I love Paul, and I realized what an idiot I'd been. Of course I'd hurt him so badly when I left him that I had some serious roads and bridges to rebuild. But he's accepted my apology. He still loves me and wants me to be his wife."

"I can't believe you didn't tell me about him." Rina placed her hand gently against her sister's lower stomach. "Or about the baby."

"I didn't want to believe it was true. You know what it was like growing up."

"Yes, I accepted Jacob's proposal for the very same reasons. He was safe. I didn't want to run the risk of—" she flung her hands in the air "—feeling like this."

"You poor baby. But don't worry. We'll pack all our stuff and be out of here as soon as we can. There's a flight to Perpignan later this afternoon. We can be on it and you can meet Paul and everything will be okay, you'll see."

Rina wished she could believe in her sister's optimistic point of view, but even knowing her sister had finally found her happiness, Rina knew she would never recover from the searing pain that filled her mind and her heart.

While they cleared their things and finished packing, made up the bed and emptied out the refrigerator, they discussed Sara's pregnancy, which had been a breeze so far. By the time the taxi arrived outside the cottage, Rina knew that at least she'd have something to look forward to. A niece or nephew to spoil and love—and to distract her from the empty sense of loss she carried deep inside her.

They'd just wheeled their cases out to the taxi when a cloud of dust came down the road. A cloud of dust accompanied by an all too familiar growl of high-performance motoring.

"He's probably just come to make sure we're leaving," Sara said. She stood in front of Rina as Rey alighted from his car. "You needn't have bothered coming to check on us. We're leaving Isla Sagrado for good."

Rey slid his expensive sunglasses off his face and took another step closer. "You might be leaving, but Sarina is most definitely not."

"I have no reason for staying here. In fact, you couldn't pay me to stay a minute longer," Rina said, and opened the back door on the taxi. "Come on, Sara. We don't want to miss our flight."

The two women got into the backseat, but before the driver could close the trunk of the car, they heard Rey bark an order in Spanish.

"Did he just tell him to take my case out of there?" Rina asked her sister.

Not waiting for a reply, she jumped out of the taxi. "What do you think you're doing? Put my case back in there."

"The *señor*, he asked me to take it out," the taxi driver said, looking uncomfortably between both Rey and Rina.

"Well, you can put it straight back in."

She stepped forward to do it herself, but at the same time, so did Rey. Her fingers tangled with his on the handle of the case.

"Please. Listen to me," he said with a quiet intensity that thrummed along her veins.

Even after everything he'd said and done to her, her body still leaped to life at his touch. She snatched her hand away, closed her eyes for a moment and swallowed against the tangle of words that lodged in her throat. She couldn't trust herself to speak.

"Rina?" Sara called as she exited the car.

"It's okay. Let him say what he has to say, then we'll go," Rina answered.

"Thank you," Rey said. "Can we go inside, for some privacy?"

"No." Rina shook her head emphatically. "Whatever you have to say to me you can say in front of my sister, as well."

"So be it." Rey nodded, but gave the ogling taxi driver a fierce look that sent the man back behind the wheel of the cab so he would not be able to hear. "I've treated you abominably."

"Yes, you have."

"I've come to beg your forgiveness."

"I don't know if I can do that. You played with me, with my feelings for you. You hurt me." Rina's voice wobbled and she saw a shaft of pain streak across Rey's face at her words.

"I know. I was proud and angry but that is no excuse—I should never have treated you so. I recognized you were different, right from the start but I refused to listen to my heart. I'd been attracted to Sara when I met her, but it was nothing compared to how I felt when I met you. The instant we were together, you completed me. Offered me calm when I most needed it. Lit a fire in me when before, the most I'd ever felt with any woman was a mild fascination. Yet despite that, I pursued my agenda without considering what it would do to you—or what it would do to me.

"It doesn't excuse me but I had reason to be suspicious. Our family had a near miss with a money-hunting opportunist only six months ago. A woman I'd allowed in my employ, thereby making my family as vulnerable to her schemes as she'd planned on making me. It very nearly cost us a small fortune, and I vowed it would never happen again. So when I realized you and Sara had exchanged places, my immediate thought was that you were taking up where the last one had failed."

"I tried to tell you, it wasn't like that," Rina said quietly.

"I know, but in my arrogance I thought I knew better. What I did was reprehensible. I chose to blur the truth with Sara when it suited me and I reacted unreasonably when faced with the very same thing in reverse. You asked me once if I lived by my family creed. I'm ashamed to say I haven't. Not for a very long time. But I aim to change that, if you'll let me."

He wiped a hand across his eyes, then looked directly at her again. She could see the sheen of tears turning his hazel eyes to green, saw the raw hope etched on his face. She didn't understand.

"Let you?" she asked. "Surely that's up to you."

He nodded. "It is up to me, but I need to be reminded from time to time of what a conceited, unfeeling ass I can be. I need someone to keep me on track, to remind me of what's most important in my life—to prevent me from falling back into the trap I've allowed myself to live in these past years. You said you loved me. Were you telling the truth?"

Rina looked at Sara who nodded. "Yes, I was."

"Then will you accept my remorse, my heart and my love?"

He dropped down onto one knee on the dusty road and pulled a ring from his pocket. A new ring, totally different from the one he'd given Sara. One Rina fell in love with almost as much as she already loved the man who offered it to her. The large central diamond—flanked by matching shoulder-set, emerald-cut stones—flashed fire in the sunlight.

"I never really understood what love was until I realized this morning that I'd sent away from me what was most true and precious in my life. Will you let me spend the rest of my life making my foolishness up to you? I love you, Sarina Woodville. Will you marry me?"

For the second time today, she heard her name on his lips and this time, it sounded as sweet as she'd ever imagined. Her heart, broken and shattered only moments ago, began to beat strong again in her chest. Hope filled her, making her light-headed, as if this wasn't real. As if she was only dreaming.

She stepped forward and knelt on the road in front of him, the stony road digging into her knees, reinforcing that she was very much awake. Tears, this time of joy, ran down her cheeks.

"Yes, I will marry you. I love you, Reynard del Castillo and don't you ever forget it."

"I won't," he promised, reaching out to wipe away her tears and to cup her face tenderly in one strong hand. "I love you. You and only you. And I will love you forever and remind you of it every single day of our life together."

He took her hand and slid the ring—her ring—upon her finger. It was a perfect fit. Then, he helped her to her feet, brushed the road dirt and grit from her knees and kissed her. It was only the sound of sniffling that drew them back to reality. Together they turned to Sara who was wiping tears of her own from her cheeks.

"Rina? Are you sure?" she asked.

"I've never been more certain of anything in my life," Rina replied.

"Then I wish you both the best of luck."

Sara dashed forward and hugged her sister tight before

doing the same with Rey. "You have a lot to live up to," she admonished. "You had better treat her right or you'll have me to answer to."

Rey smiled and looked at Rina. "Don't worry. She is my everything."

Rina and Rey stood together, arms entwined about one another, as Sara got back into the taxi and it drove away. Rey reached for Rina's suitcase and dragged it behind them as they went into the cottage.

When the door closed firmly behind them, an apparition—a woman in eighteenth century dress—straightened from the flowers she'd been tending, and smiled gently before fading away.

* * * * *

Benedict's story is next!
Don't miss FOR THE SAKE OF THE SECRET CHILD,
the enticing conclusion of Yvonne Lindsay's
WED AT ANY PRICE trilogy,
from Silhouette Desire.

COMING NEXT MONTH

Available October 12, 2010

#2041 ULTIMATUM: MARRIAGE
Ann Major
Man of the Month

#2042 TAMING HER BILLIONAIRE BOSS
Maxine Sullivan
Dynasties: The Jarrods

#2043 CINDERELLA & THE CEO
Maureen Child
Kings of California

#2044 FOR THE SAKE OF THE SECRET CHILD
Yvonne Lindsay
Wed at Any Price

#2045 SAVED BY THE SHEIKH!
Tessa Radley

#2046 FROM BOARDROOM TO WEDDING BED?
Jules Bennett

REQUEST YOUR FREE BOOKS!

2 FREE NOVELS
PLUS 2
FREE GIFTS!

Silhouette

Desire®

Passionate, Powerful, Provocative!

HARLEQUIN®

A Romance

FOR EVERY MOOD™

Spotlight on

Inspirational

Wholesome romances
that touch the heart and soul.

See the next page
to enjoy a sneak peek from
the Love Inspired® inspirational series.

Autumn Granger gave her horse rein to slide toward the town's new sheriff.

"Hey, there." The man in a brand-new Stetson, black T-shirt, jeans and riding boots held up a hand in greeting. He stepped away from his four-wheel drive with "Sheriff" in black on the doors and waded through the grasses. "I'm new around here."

"I'm Autumn Granger."

"Nice to meet you, Miss Granger. I'm Ford Sherman, from Chicago." He knuckled back his hat, revealing the most handsome face she'd ever seen. Big blue eyes contrasted with his sun-tanned complexion.

"I'm guessing you haven't seen much open land. Out here, you've got to keep an eye on cows or they're going to tear your vehicle apart."

"What?" He whipped around. Sure enough, mammoth black-and-white creatures had started to gnaw on his four-wheel drive. They clustered like a mob, mouths and tongues and teeth bent on destruction. One cow tried to pry the wiper off the windshield, another chewed on the side mirror. Several leaned through the open window, licking the seats.

"Move along, little dogie." He didn't know the first thing about cattle.

The entire herd swiveled their heads to study him curiously. Not a single hoof shifted. The animals soon returned to chewing, licking, digging through his possessions.

Autumn laughed, a warm and wonderful sound. "Thanks,

I needed that." She then pulled a bag from behind her saddle and waved it at the cows. "Look what I have, guys. Cookies."

Cows swung in her direction, and dozens of liquid brown eyes brightened with cookie hopes. As she circled the car, the cattle bounded after her. The earth shook with the force of their powerful hooves.

"Next time, you're on your own, city boy." She tipped her hat. The cowgirl stayed on his mind, the sweetest thing he had ever seen.

*Will Ford be able to stick it out in the country
to find out more about Autumn?
Find out in HIS HOLIDAY BRIDE
by bestselling author Jillian Hart,
available in October 2010
only from Love Inspired®.*

HARLEQUIN®

Texas Legacies: The McCabes

The McCabes of Texas are back!
5 new stories from popular author

CATHY GILLEN THACKER

The Triplets' First Thanksgiving
(October 2010)

Paige Chamberlain desperately wants to be a mother…
but helping former rival Kurt McCabe raise three
abandoned babies isn't quite what she had in mind.
There's going to be a full house at the McCabe
residence this holiday season!

Also watch for
A Cowboy under the Mistletoe *(December 2010)*

"LOVE, HOME & HAPPINESS"

www.eHarlequin.com

HAR75329